Carlton Dawe

Kakemonos

Tales of the Far East

Carlton Dawe

Kakemonos
Tales of the Far East

ISBN/EAN: 9783337082154

Printed in Europe, USA, Canada, Australia, Japan

Cover: Foto ©Andreas Hilbeck / pixelio.de

More available books at **www.hansebooks.com**

KAKEMONOS
TALES OF THE
FAR EAST
BY W. CARLTON DAWE

JOHN LANE: THE BODLEY HEAD

LONDON AND NEW YORK, 1897

Printed by T. and A. CONSTABLE, Printers to Her Majesty

CONTENTS

ON THE BANKS OF THE MENAM

THE voyage up the Gulf of Siam had been an uneventful one, and we had no sooner cast anchor off the island of Koh-si-chang than I was all impatience to be away sight-seeing at Bangkok. But our ship being too big to go up the Menam, we perforce had to wait for the small steamer which plies between the island and the capital, unless we cared about venturing a voyage in one of the rice-boats. This latter alternative not being to our way of thinking, we decided to await the steamer; so, the next morning after breakfast, we got out one of the ship's boats and pulled ashore in search of game. In those days there were only a couple of native huts on Koh-si-chang, the half-clothed inhabitants of which rolled out to gaze with wonder upon the white invaders. It is with surprise I hear that the king has since built a summer palace there,

A

and that at certain seasons of the year the desolate little island is astir with the great ones of the land.

However, at daybreak of the following morning we boarded the little steamer, which had duly arrived during the night, and which lay-to alongside of us for the purpose, and away we went for the capital. Our captain was a long, thin Englishman with a dark, untrimmed beard, who had spent the best twenty years of his life in that enervating region, and who now appeared so attenuated and feeble that you found yourself wondering how he managed to hold together. The only other European on board was the engineer, a sturdy Scot, who dined with us in his greasy singlet and read Goethe in German betweenwhiles. He too had spent the best years of his life loafing about the coast ; but the climate, or his greasy profession, seemed to agree very well with him, for to me he appeared a substantially built man, and he ate heartily of the curious-smelling food which the native cook provided.

After we had crossed the bar the real interest of the journey began. We passed the Paknam fortifications, which in after years were to fail so lamentably before a third-rate French gun-boat, but which the natives thought effectually secured them against invasion from the sea. Here and there the curious-shaped *wats*, or temples, towered up out of the thick jungle, while numbers of yellow-robed priests passing up and down the river lent movement and variety to the scene. Here a blue-funnel boat, bound for Singapore, forged slowly past us through the thick water; there, a little higher up, we met a Scottish Oriental, deep-laden, bound for Hong-Kong. The further up we advanced the busier grew the scene; and when at length we made fast to a buoy in mid-stream, we appeared to be in the centre of the shipping industry. To be sure, there was no 'forest of masts,' but nevertheless there was apparently a consider-able trade done.

The rest of that day was spent in driving through the city, and after dinner that same evening we went, in company with a fellow from the British consulate, to see the sights of the town. He was a good sort, was well known, and consequently well received; but of the things we saw, or of the things we did, I have no inten-tion of speaking—that is, with one exception.

Our peregrinations happened to bring us within the vicinity of the native theatre and the clash of tom-toms. Then our consular friend suddenly started, like one remembering an important thing, and suggested a visit to the native abode of Thespis. Without more ado we agreed, and as we walked along he informed us that the performers were really the slaves of a wealthy nobleman, who allowed them to appear in this public capacity two or three times every year.

I shouldn't like to be forced to tell what the play was about, having but a hazy recollection of it all. There was a considerable number of large-limbed women who kicked up their heels and displayed their naked shoulders to advantage, and there was one triple-crowned contortionist, evidently the 'star,' who came in for the lion's share of the applause. It was in its way exceedingly clever, and one should only judge things according to their pretensions. I confess I didn't care much for it myself, though I must also admit that our friend from the consulate seemed to think it a remarkably fine exhibition.

His official standing had enabled us to get

fairly close to the big square which did duty for a stage, while the position I occupied was not many feet from the performers. Indeed, when the *corps de ballet* filled the scene, one of its most prominent members was very near to me.

Yes, it all happened very quickly. I first noted her gaudy yellow dress, then her bare arms and shoulders. I thought she looked pale in the artificial light, perhaps a little tired or ill; but her eyes shone into mine with an intenseness quite bewildering. She was a grand girl, standing firmly on her feet, and carrying her head as though it were the rarest jewel in the world. Though, under all circumstances, a scrupulously conscientious man, I was not one to turn away when a lady looked at me. I therefore did my best to appease her curiosity. That she was extremely curious there could be little doubt, for whenever she came on the stage her great black eyes sought me out, and when I smiled she smiled, at first in a nervous, hesitating way, as though she feared some one would see her. Indeed, I was afterwards told that the ladies were watched with a vigilance peculiar to the East; but as I looked upon the eye-making as merely a momentary joke, I did not display that discretion which the circumstances really warranted.

'Do you see that woman?' I whispered to my consular friend, nodding towards the divinity in old gold.

'See her!' he laughed. 'Egad, I've done nothing but see her lately! At first I thought she was looking at me, but, by George, it's another dog altogether!'

'What do you think of her, eh?'

'Oh,' he answered indifferently, and, I thought, a little spitefully, 'you won't notice her teeth in the dark.'

I laughed. 'She's got a pair of shoulders, though.'

'Most women have.'

'And an ankle.'

'A common failing of the sex.'

'Get out! But no larks, now.'

'Restrain your ardour, my dear fellow. Her ankles are as far beyond your reach as though she were in heaven.'

'I don't know.'

'You're not likely to. It's true, all the same. My dear fellow, this woman is one of Prince Krum's beauties. Who the devil is Prince

Krum? Only a cousin of the king, and one of the richest men in the country. Guarded? I should think they are. Spies everywhere. You see that fat old chap with the womanish face?—that one over there, the one with the little red cap. No, don't point. There, he's looking at you now. Well, he's the guardian of this bevy of beauty. I know him quite well by sight, the beastly old eunuch!'

This piece of information startled me somewhat, for I had been watching this old man for a considerable time, wondering why he stared so persistently at me. I turned to the girl and caught her eyes, and, as if my brain transferred its thought to hers, she immediately began to study the pattern of the carpet. I thought I saw a peculiar smile break across the swollen face of the eunuch. I know I felt decidedly foolish and uncomfortable.

'Better give it up, old man,' said my consular friend encouragingly, as we emerged from the theatre. 'Trust Krum for taking good care of his pet birds.'

'Damn Krum!'

'With pleasure; but that won't drag those ankles out of heaven.'

Then he patted me affably on the back, told me to cheer up, and otherwise endeavoured to console me with a chattering stream of ridicule. I bore it all good-naturedly enough, the incident not having yet attained a serious interest. Moreover, I had noted a tone of pique in his voice, and this rendered me complaisant. He could not forgive the girl for her lamentable lack of taste.

And yet I was not so sure, should I feel inclined to press the adventure further, that the girl was as far beyond me as he pretended. True, I hadn't the remotest knowledge of her whereabouts, nor had I formed any plan which might enable me to discover her; and yet I had a half-belief, a sort of intuition, that I should meet her again, if only in heaven. I, however, refrained from acquainting my sceptical friend with this belief. Being utterly devoid of sentiment, he would not have understood me, and there is nothing more trying to exaltation than contemptible commonplaces.

We returned to our hotel by boat, and an extremely pleasant journey it was down the moonlit river. My companions chatted away merrily, while now and again our jovial guide tipped us a stave of a popular song. He was a merry dog, and his merriment proved catching. Trying to persuade myself that my pretty little adventure was mercilessly nipped in the bud, I did my best to banish the girl from my thoughts, lit a cigar, and lent a robust voice to the chorus which rolled noisily over the white, soft bosom of the Menam.

But our friend from the consulate had forgotten to apprise us of the fact that the city of Bangkok boasts an extremely singular product known as the 'hat-snatcher,' a person who plies his trade in the most open and barefaced manner. What a half-naked coolie could do with European hats when stolen would at first seem something of a problem ; but as there are thousands of pawnshops in the city, mostly owned by Chinese, no doubt he finds a ready market. The Chinaman, on the other hand, is much too clever to buy anything he can't get rid of at a good profit.

It was the morning after our visit to the theatre, and we arose with the intention of further exploring the city. As I stepped out from the hotel and looked up and down the river, a coolie in a flaring loin-cloth came within my line of vision, but, being only a coolie, his presence occasioned no surprise. Indeed, so little attention did I pay him that I started suddenly when I found him whining at my side. One hand was outstretched in a nervous manner, and between his brown fingers he held a slip of red paper like a Chinese visiting-card. He spoke rapidly, and in a low, earnest tone, but of course I could not understand a syllable he uttered. Thinking, however, that he was begging, and wishing to get rid of him, I flung him a small coin and bade him be off; but instead of picking up the money he shook his head, advanced a step nearer me, and began speaking more earnestly than ever. Not knowing what the fellow's object could be, I raised my stick threateningly and drove him back. I was never quite sure whether the look that leapt into his eyes at this action was one of anger or regret; but of one thing I am sure, and that is that he hung his head dejectedly as I turned away and re-entered the hotel.

Upon emerging a few minutes later I looked round for him, but he was nowhere to be seen, and, prompted by curiosity, I walked over to the spot where he had approached me. To my surprise I saw the coin still glittering on the ground, and for some inexplicable reason left it there.

But out in the road, by the fence of the French consulate, I again saw the same coolie, who salaamed as solemnly as before. I don't know how it happened, but I found myself salaaming in return, and then to my infinite relief the carriage dashed on citywards.

I thought no more of the matter till my companion drew my attention to the fact that the man was following us. Under ordinary circumstances such an occurrence might be deemed unimportant, as droves of whining beggars invariably follow the European; but this man I knew to be no beggar. What was he, then?

I turned round in my seat so as to get a better look at him, but all these coolies seem so much alike that it requires a trained eye to pick out any peculiarity of gait or feature. He came along easily enough, the sun flashing on his bare body. When he saw me looking he stopped dead, salaamed respectfully, and then came on again. I waved indignantly for him to go away, but he paid no heed to the protest.

'What persistent brutes they are!' said my companion. 'That fellow 'll cling to our heels till he gets what he wants.'

'Yes.'

But I did not like to say how strangely the man's presence affected me; nor, for some absurd reason, did I mention aught concerning my previous interview with him. Who was he? what was he? A spy, a thief, or a possible murderer? I own to being most unaccountably puzzled, nor was I without a certain sort of anxiety. And yet I did not think the man was either a thief or a murderer, though he could be following me for no good reason.

Full of curious conjecture, I threw myself back on the seat and tried hard to listen to the glib remarks of my companion, who was humorously dilating on the many original characteristics of the native at home, though to my way of thinking he cuts a much more comical figure abroad.

We had by this time entered the well-packed native quarter. Here innumerable streets branched off in all directions. The road was crowded with naked children and half-naked men and women, but with a flourish of his whip and a hoarse shout our driver was in among them, scattering them, clacking like a flock of geese. It was at that moment I felt a sudden lightness in the region of my head, and on putting up my hand I found my hat was gone.

'Hi! stop, stop!'

The words were scarcely out of my mouth before we had pulled up with a clatter in the midst of the rabble. Springing to my feet and looking over the back of the trap, I saw, with a feeling akin to nervousness, that the person who had thus unceremoniously relieved me of my headgear was my friend the coolie. I motioned for him to advance, but instead of doing so he defiantly waved the prize above his head, as though challenging me to come and fetch it.

'I guessed he was up to no good,' said my companion consolingly. 'The chap's a thief.'

It needed no great puzzling of the brain to arrive at that conclusion. If I hadn't been a fool I might have known it long before.

Our coachman, whom we had heard mutter an occasional word of broken English, here ejaculated, 'Yessir—'at thief.'

I sprang from the carriage and made as though I would accept the rogue's challenge, but he no sooner saw me advance than he dashed down one of the numerous alleys with inconceivable speed.

'No good,' cried my companion, 'come back. You'd lose sight of him before you'd gone a hundred yards.'

Feeling the truth of this, I reluctantly returned, longing with an unchristian ardour to lay my hands upon the heathen's body.

Pushing my way through the grinning crowd, I managed to make the driver understand that I wished to purchase a new hat. 'Yessir, oh, yessir,' he replied, and waving his whip aloft he screamed shrilly at the people, who, displaying much wisdom, rapidly fell back. As the excitable little pony plunged forward I took a last look round, and there at the top of the alley-way stood my friend the coolie swinging my new *terai* above his head.

Our friend from the consulate dined with us that night, and during the meal some one incidentally referred to my adventure of the morning. The consul laughed.

'Awfully sorry I forgot to tell you,' he said, 'but hat-snatching is a very lucrative profession here in Bangkok. It's odd, though, that the beggar should have waited as he did and almost invite pursuit. It's usually a snatch and a dash down some alley almost before you have time to catch your breath. I assure you I never heard of anything like it.'

'That is the least singular part of the affair,' I answered. Then I told them all how the thief had come to me in the morning, how he had left the coin lying on the ground, and how he had subsequently followed the carriage.

The man from the consulate opened his eyes.

'Singular, indeed,' he said. 'I confess I can't quite make it out. By the way, do you carry a revolver?'

'I have one, though I never carry it.'

'If I were you I should while I remained in Bangkok.'

'You don't mean——'

'I don't mean anything, old chap. You'll feel more secure, that's all.'

That night I locked my door before going to

bed, and in my half-waking moments I had blurred visions of a brown-skinned coolie careering madly along the dusty roads, under a column of many-coloured hats as high as the dome of St. Paul's.

On entering the room next morning I should not have been at all surprised to find that my rascally friend had called on me, or left a card intimating where I might pick up second-hand hats very cheap. I was quite prepared to believe that the fellow was capable of any impertinence; and when I found that he had not condescended to call, my disappointment was extreme. He was not even out on the frontage by the river, a state of things which suggested a fly and an immediate setting out in search of him. But, joking apart, the mysterious behaviour of the man had appealed to me in spite of my better reason. There was a sense of suggestion, of incompleteness, about the whole business which prevented me from passing on to other things; and try as I would I could not banish from my mind the man or his singular behaviour. What that behaviour portended I had not the remotest idea. I had my own doubts as to his wish to inflict bodily harm on me, for, unless the man were mad, how could he wish to injure one against whom he could possibly have no grudge? Nevertheless, I took the advice of my friend from the consulate about carrying a revolver. There is much wisdom in a state of readiness.

That night we attended the magnificent ceremony of the burning of the king's mother. She had died some months previously, and her son, having grown weary of sackcloth and ashes, had given the order for her cremation. Even the death of a queen must not entirely retard the progress of a nation. There were grand doings in the neighbourhood of the crematorium, which had been specially built for the illustrious dead ; and as I and my companions wandered in and out amid the throng, which showed up luridly by the fitful glare of the sputtering torches, I suddenly missed them, and for a moment or two stood irresolute looking to right and left. As I did so a native passed swiftly beside me, and so closely that I could almost swear he touched me. He took half a dozen quick steps, and then, swinging round on his heel, came towards me with a soft, swift, gliding movement. Indeed, by the indifferent light, and dressed in white as he was, he seemed more like a spectre than a man. Not yet sure that it was I he sought, and failing to attach anything of importance to his movements, I seemed only half-aware of his proximity before he was upon me. Then like a flash he passed to the right of me and I felt my hat go.

Springing round with an oath, I savagely grasped my revolver, but was only in time to see a white figure mingle with a group of other white figures. Nothing daunted, I walked on in the direction the thief had taken, and presently seeing a form, which I thought resembled his, detach itself from the group, I kept it in sight. Of course I made no pretence of hurrying, not wishing to alarm the fellow, or cause a disturbance; and yet it was curious how that figure kept its distance from me. Whether I walked slow or fast, attempted a little run or a double, the thing was always before me like my shadow.

At last it led me to the top of a narrow, dark street, and, seeing me hesitate, it also hesitated. I was strongly tempted to pursue the thing, though my better sense warned me of the folly of so doing. What could I hope to gain by such an adventure? I did not even know that the fellow was the one who had stolen my hat. And yet my temperament was such that I knew nothing but a solving of the mystery would satisfy me.

But here all doubts as to the identity of the man were set at rest, for seeing me hesitate, and fearing I would give up the pursuit, he boldly advanced to within a few yards of me and waved my hat in my face. I immediately sprang forward, hoping to seize him, but he was off with surprising agility, I after him. But a few yards of such going were enough to convince me of the danger of running in such a place, and at once slackening down I pursued him more leisurely. Apparently unconcerned, he too slackened his speed, and, keeping about a dozen yards ahead, he led me right through the dark, evil-smelling street.

Quite convinced now that the man was no ordinary thief, I was determined to see the adventure through. Perhaps I had my doubts about the wisdom of such an act, but my curiosity was stronger than my discretion. I had not the remotest idea where, or to what, the man was leading me ; but in those days I had plenty of faith in myself, and perhaps not a little in my six-shooter. At any rate, I loosened that weapon and kept it ready to my hand, and left the rest to chance.

After traversing the aforementioned dirty street, my guide bore round to the left, and presently I thought I recognised on the other side of the road the walls of the barracks ; but, without stopping, the fellow led me to the right and then to the left, up one street and down another, till I abandoned all hope of fixing my whereabouts : though, by what I could make out of the surroundings, I seemed to be in a more substantially built part of the town.

Presently I found myself walking in the shadow of a high wall, my guide still the same distance before me. Something told me that we were approaching our destination, and instinctively my feet slipped less noisily over the ground. Then I saw my guide stop and hold up his hand, and, scarcely knowing what I did, I obeyed the gesture. Yet from where I stood I could see him fumbling about, apparently with the wall : then all of a sudden he disappeared.

Startled a little, I once more felt for my revolver, the touch of the steel having a re-assuring effect on my agitated nerves. Then after waiting for half a minute or so to see if he would reappear, I advanced to the spot where I had last seen him, and behold, the cause of his vanishing was instantly explained. There was a stout wooden doorway let into the wall, and through this the spectre had passed.

I stood waiting, wondering, uncertain whether to advance or retreat. Thought upon thought counselling the utmost prudence pleaded with considerable eloquence : but in the hands of men and women prudence is like a piece of elastic, and may be conscientiously stretched to suit the occasion. The wall was grim, the door suspicious. In the open street there might be a chance, but behind that wall what hope was there for one man if mischief were meant him? And yet I was loth to forgo the adventure at what seemed to be its most critical point. Uncertainty there was in abundance, danger there might be, but I must get to the bottom of the business ; and so, without more ado, I put my hand to the gate and pushed. It moved a little, but on pushing harder it opened wide enough to allow me to slip through. This I did without further hesitation.

For a few moments I stood on the steps which led down from the gate, and peered intently into the darkness. That I was in some private grounds, or garden, I easily guessed, though the light that stole through the trees was fitful in the extreme. But presently out of the shadows the white form of my coolie friend appeared, and I immediately descended the steps and drew near. As I advanced the fellow salaamed most humbly, muttering beneath his breath something in an apologetic tone. Then with a still more elaborate bow he handed me my hat, and turning on his heel beckoned me to follow. This I did with alacrity, for I now began to wonder strange things.

But after going a few yards he stopped suddenly, uttered a low exclamation of annoyance, and then retraced his steps, motioning for me to do likewise. Wondering what new turn events had suddenly taken, I slipped my hand in my pocket, felt my revolver, and kept close to his heels. Unnecessary prudence.

The fellow had merely forgotten to lock the gate. I came suspiciously close as he did so, but, instead of evincing any concern, he took pains to show me how the thing was done. A heavy beam of wood, slipped through a huge staple in the door, and then into a recess in the wall, composed the mechanism; and though the ceremony interested me but little, the act of the coolie awoke in me renewed confidence. He grunted with satisfaction as the bar shot into its place, and then turning about motioned as before for me to follow him.

Down the narrow, smooth path we went, the man in his bare feet gliding noiselessly before me, I slipping along almost as quietly. Above, through the thin trees, I caught an occasional glimmer from the feeble stars, but, there being no moon, the night was very dark. And darker it grew all of a sudden, for without warning I found myself in the deep shadow of a huge mass of masonry. A house, I guessed, though whether it was house or wall I could not tell. Here my guide touched me gently on the arm and murmured something that seemed like a warning. I drew back a step further amid the shrubs that grew alongside the masonry, and with eyes and ears alert awaited the next move.

I saw my friend the coolie flit hither and thither, noiselessly as a ghost ; now he bent this way, now that, and, as far as I could make out, he was listening intently. But if he expected to hear anything he was disappointed, for nothing but the rustling of the leaves overhead, and an occasional moan of the wind, came to relieve the oppressive stillness. Then he came to me, and seizing me by the hand led me a few steps to the right, and then halted before a low door. This he opened noiselessly, and without more ado we entered, the man softly closing the door behind him.

We were now in complete darkness, and I began to entertain visions of traps, assassinations, and sundry other curious and alarming pictures ; but the man still held my hand, and my pride forbade me to show any sign of doubt or fear. My forethought, however, had enabled me to give him my left hand, which allowed me to keep the right within easy reach of my revolver. I had fully made up my mind that if anything untoward happened, my coolie friend should pay for it. Perhaps he paid dearly enough for it in the end, but in quite another way.

Despite the lightness of my tread, my footsteps rang hollowly as we walked, which proclaimed the nature of our path ; but presently those hollow sounds died away, and I felt my feet touch some soft carpet or matting. Here my conductor slipped from my side, and fearing some treachery I stepped back several paces till I felt the wall. I admit to the moment or two of suspense which followed, and then I noticed a feeble light to the left of me. It was the coolie who advanced with a small lamp in his hand.

Signalling me to follow him in silence, he led the way across the room, the outlines of which I could but indistinctly discern, at the further end of which hung a pair of heavy curtains. Parting these he disclosed a narrow staircase which led upward, and then stood aside holding the curtains for me to pass. I looked at him suspiciously, but he only smiled reassuringly and motioned for me to advance. Advance, yes, but where, to what? Again the fellow smiled, and again my instinct told me to trust him, though prudence cautioned me with no uncertain voice. And then I almost laughed aloud as I thought. Prudence! what had I to do with such a quality? The moment I had given myself into the keeping of this coolie, prudence and I had parted company. Come what might I would see the thing through.

Up the stairs I went, the man holding the light above his head for me to see, and in a brief space I reached the top. Then the light was withdrawn, but I was no longer in darkness, for away before me, at the end of what appeared to be a long passage, I beheld a feeble glimmer. Towards this I immediately set out, my pulses now going at express speed. The air was warm here, and scented, and seemed to intoxicate me as I drew it in. Over the thick carpet my feet slipped noiselessly, and with a rapidity born of intense excitement I approached the lamp. It was then I saw that the passage apparently ended in a blind wall, but on getting closer I discovered that the supposed wall was a pair of heavy dark curtains which hung rigidly in their place.

That the lamp was meant as a guide I could not doubt, and yet I stood irresolute before those curtains wondering what the next step would lead to. Then with a conscious throb of irritation I drew the curtains aside, and——

The room was low, dimly lighted, and full of rich perfume, the perfume that had almost made me drunk. Here and there were grim Oriental carvings, the designs of which cut fantastic capers in the strange light, and here and there were quaint Oriental seats, and hangings of curious designs in silver and gold. The light stole through the pink globe of a lamp which hung in the far corner, beneath which I saw a woman reclining amid a heap of rosy cushions. By the way her breast rose and fell I guessed she was asleep, though her manner of waking as I advanced, and her affected cry of alarm when she beheld me, gave me that confidence I might otherwise have lacked.

I bowed, drawing still nearer to her, muttering an apology for my intrusion, which, of course, she didn't understand, but which made not the slightest difference to me. Training demanded an expression of some sort, and if the lady didn't know what I meant she had not the usual acumen of her sex.

She rose as I advanced, and I recognised her in a moment. It was the same woman whom

I had seen dancing in the native theatre. She wore the same yellow dress : great gold bangles spanned her wrists and ankles, those ankles which, after all, were not so far off as heaven. She smiled as she saw I recognised her, and murmured something in a soft, low voice. I answered, and she listened intently while I spoke ; but when I finished she shook her head with a pathetic little smile. Yet under some conditions the eyes speak more eloquently than the tongue, and those conditions were with us at that moment.

.   .   .   .   .   .

And so for the next three nights my coolie friend met me at the gate and escorted me to the bottom of the stairs as he had done on the occasion of my first visit. But on the fourth night there was no coolie escort awaiting me, though when I pushed the gate I found to my relief that it had been left unlocked. Though evidently called away on some other business, he had arranged everything for my easy entrance. Knowing the road so well by this time, I soon passed down the garden and entered the house by the little low door. Here I stood for several seconds listening intently ; but no sound of a suspicious nature reaching me, I pursued my way.

The woman was waiting for me as before ; the coffee in dainty little cups was spread on the richly inlaid table, the sweetmeats piled in dainty dishes beside it. She let an unconscious sigh of relief escape her as she saw me, and I thought she clung to me rather hysterically. Her big eyes shone excitedly, and nothing could assuage the rise and fall of her breast.

It happened like a flash. There was a sudden swish of the curtains to the right of us, and half a dozen men bounded into the apartment —mercenaries, I did not doubt. As I sprang to my feet and faced them they drew their knives as one man—long, ugly weapons like Malay creeses —and threatened me with instant annihilation. But finding the ferocity of their looks ineffectual, one of the men advanced a step, pointed to the woman, and said something. What it was I did not know, but I guessed easily enough. He wanted me to hand her over. The poor thing shrank trembling to my side and turned a pair of imploring eyes into mine. Had I been the most selfish of mortals I could not have resisted that mute appeal. I knew enough of the inner life of the East to guess the fate of faithless women ; and recognising my obligations, I shook my head at the men and flung one arm round the quivering shoulders of the woman.

This act was answered in just the way I expected. It was the signal for an immediate advance on the part of the enemy ; but as they raised their feet for the second step, I brought my pistol to bear full on the leader's face. For a moment he did not seem to recognise the weapon, but when he did he fell back with a cry of rage. The others huddled together in a heap behind him, and seemed to be in deadly terror lest I should let fly. But such was not my intention unless close pressed : then it was a case of save himself who could.

Seeing the marked effect my revolver had upon them, I resolved to test its moral influence to the full. Acting upon that excellent intent, I moved slowly towards the curtain through which I had entered, still keeping the woman by my side. When close pressed, and in desperate straits, we must, if we would fight our way out, think quickly and act with boldness and precision. It was evident that I could not leave the woman to the mercy of those hired ruffians ; it was also evident that I could not expect to remain long in that place without violence of some sort being directed against me. True, I didn't know where I could take her, or what I should do for her if rescued. Indeed, I never thought anything about it. My one fixed idea was to save her from the fury of her persecutors.

They watched my movements with stealthy glances, my boldness not a little disconcerting them ; but, as I had their captain covered, and as he feared to move, none of the others attempted an advance. On the contrary, three of them retreated slowly till they were right against the curtain which shielded their entrance, and as I watched I saw them disappear behind it. For a moment, but for a moment only, I congratulated myself. Then I knew that another and a worse danger threatened me. The three men whom I thought my pistol had terrified had either gone to alarm the house or to cut off my retreat. This fact the woman seemed to grasp as soon as I. She uttered a quick exclamation and pointed excitedly to the exit.

Immediately turning my attention to it I began a cautious if quick retreat; but our assailants, fearful that we should make good our escape before their companions intercepted us, bounded forward as at a given signal. I fired full at the leader, but in the excitement missed my aim, or, at least, did nothing but tear a hole through his ear. With a howl of pain he sprang at me, and, though I brought him to the floor with my second shot, he ran his knife into my thigh as he fell. Then, like a pair of devils, the other two were upon me, and though I fired once, twice, I failed to hit them in any vital part. A knife flashed before my eyes—indeed, it seemed to be almost in my face before I saw it. And yet my hand went up, and the sharp steel rang on the barrel of my revolver, knocking that weapon from my hand. The man immediately closed with me, and then began a fierce struggle to see which should throttle the other.

Round and round the room we went, sending a table spinning here, a bench there, I moving rapidly with the object of giving the other fellow no opportunity of striking me. He circled round and round me with his weapon ready to stab, I using as best I could his companion as a shield. But at length, being pressed close, I stumbled over a low divan, and both I and my opponent went flying to the floor.

Now began a struggle to see, not which should get uppermost, but which should secure the bottom place; for like a flash of inspiration came the warning that the underneath position would be the safer. Unfortunately, in falling, I had thought only of getting my opponent beneath me, and this, to my confusion, I succeeded in doing. It was when I wished to reverse this state of things that the struggle came. But it did not last long. With a quick movement the fellow caught me by the arms; I saw his companion dash forward; I almost fancied I could feel the knife entering my back. Instead of that there came a sharp, agonising shriek, and the would-be assassin lurched forward on his face some three or four yards away. Surprised, I threw my opponent off and sprang to my feet, and behold! the woman was my deliverer. There she stood with the dripping knife in her hand, a look of fearful exultation in her eyes. She saw the look of gratitude in mine, and her wild face brightened.

C

But there was no time for words, nor looks neither. Stooping, I picked up my revolver, and also possessed myself of my would-be assassin's knife. As for the fellow with whom I had wrestled, there was nothing further to fear from him. He was lying insensible, with mouth and eyes open, breathing stertorously. With a quick gesture I called the woman to my side, and together we quitted the chamber.

Beyond the curtain the passage was in darkness, but the woman seized my hand and hurriedly led me forward. Knowing every inch of the way as she did, I could not have had a better guide. Onward we went over the soft carpet at a rapid pace, down the stairs of which I have already spoken, and so on through the passage in which I recollected that my steps echoed strangely. Then, almost before I was aware we had reached it, she flung open the low door which gave admittance to the house, and, ere I could restrain her, sprang out into the grounds. At the same moment three white forms flitted out from the surrounding shadows, and three cruel knives went stab, stab, stab into her bare breast. With scarcely a moan she fell back in my arms the blood gushing out from the three separate wounds. That the blows were meant for me I did not doubt, and at that moment I almost regretted that the assassins had made a mistake.

Lifting the poor girl's head in my arms, I tried to staunch the awful flow of blood ; but she was already in the last fearful gasp. Even as I held her head I felt it grow suddenly heavy.

The assassins, having done their work, fled I know not whither. Without further molestation I reached the gate, passed out, and left the dead girl to the care of the gods.

HIS JAPANESE WIFE

SO-CALLED men of honour are notoriously dis-
honourable where women are concerned. As
man to man they savour much of self-sufficiency;
as man to woman they wear quite another coat.
But in the Far East such things matter little,
and the native woman doesn't count. She may
have a soul to save, but we doubt it. Heaven
knows, her own men think little enough of
her: we think less. She may have brothers
and sisters, a mother—a husband, perchance.
It is really no affair of ours. To those who
stay at home in England and sentimentally
ponder over the magnificent self-sacrifice of
the missionaries, their loyalty, steadfastness,
and devotion to a hopeless cause, the life of the
ordinary young fellow in the East may come
as something of a shock. But trust the ordinary
young fellow for knowing what he is about.
When he do n't, he makes what the world
calls a hideous failure of his life.

36

Cuthbertson was such a failure, and those who knew him are never likely to tread in his steps. Nobility is a transcendent virtue when it doesn't cost you anything : in Cuthbertson's case it was a deplorable vice. The preacher will tell us that we are all brothers : he knows very well that we are nothing of the kind. Custom is a barrier through which the blood of brotherhood may trickle, but which it can never surmount. Nor need we go to the East to find comparisons.

Cuthbertson was what is commonly called a 'good sort'—in the best sense of the term. The man, without being in the least degree priggish, was thoroughly honest ; and if he never indulged in our excesses, he could take his whisky-and-soda with the best of us. A spruce, tidy fellow, with a thoughtful dark face and a pair of exceedingly pathetic eyes. I confess I always had a sneaking regard for him ; and though some of the younger fellows thought he gave himself superior airs, I think I understood him. The difference between us was merely one of balance : of course we knew on whose side the deficiency lay.

So far he had managed to steer pretty clear

of the women, which, to our way of thinking, was anything but an agreeable sign.   Nor did we forget to let him know it : but he only shook his head and smiled.   The pathetic eyes may have looked a shade more pathetic : for the rest, the man was unassailable.

As a rule he sat at the head of our mess, and I must admit that, undemonstrative as he was, his presence acted beneficially upon us. There were no assumed airs, no little bits of consequence peeping out ; but all the same we knew that Cuthbertson's eyes were upon us, and we guessed that the brain behind was summing us up, and not unfairly.   There was at least one man in Yokohama who had the whip-hand of our human frailties.

Then came the night when he suddenly announced his intention of severing his con-nection with the mess, and very politely requested us to elect another chairman.   He was going to move into new quarters, he said, and begged that we would sometimes give him a kindly thought.   Of course we drank his health and declared that he was the jolliest of jolly fellows ; and he made a very neat and suitable speech, to which two or three of our members attempted a reply; but Cuthbertson's easy effort put their stammering to the blush.

The next night his chair was empty. Much as we, in a silent way, resented his superiority, I think we missed him a good deal when he left—more, in fact, than any of us would care to admit; but we elected another chairman in his place, and the world went on spinning just the same.

In the meantime it leaked out that he had taken a neat little cottage on the Bluff, and that he had a pretty little Jap to keep house for him. Of course we smiled significantly at the latter piece of information, surprised and yet not surprised; though we protested that he had stolen a most unjustifiable march upon us. And yet I think he went up several degrees in our estimation. We like other fellows to possess our own manly attributes.

He bore the subsequent chaff well enough. Sometimes I thought he flushed painfully, at others his curious brown eyes flashed sudden sparks of fire—real resentful fire that almost seemed to scorch. But that was when the remarks ran too freely on the housekeeper.

After all, it was nobody's business but his own, and a man's housekeeper need not necessarily be old and ugly. Accident may occasionally unearth a fairly presentable one, and when it does, what is man that he should run counter to the gods? We, however, failed most lamentably in our endeavours to get an introduction. Cuthbertson smiled affably enough at the suggestion, and even went so far as to say that he would see about it ; but we knew that he never entertained the notion for a moment. It was always, 'Some day, old chap '—the day that never comes.

Perhaps it was scarcely consistent with our exalted notions of honour, but we determined by hook or by crook to get a peep at Cuthbertson's mysterious housekeeper. We thought, apart from our knowledge of the uses to which housekeepers are put, that there was something underhand in this particular engagement ; but for a long time the secret, if there were one, baffled us. None of us was ever asked to the cottage to dinner, though occasionally a fellow from the office went up to tiffin. But eyes were strained in vain, ears kept vainly on the alert. The housekeeper knew how to send in a good tiffin, and also how to keep herself out of sight.

But one Sunday afternoon, happening to be in the neighbourhood of the cottage, I thought I would look Cuthbertson up and give him the time of the day. Filled with this friendly intention, I approached the house. His boy met me on the verandah, and in answer to my inquiries informed me that his master had just gone out, but that he was expected back every moment. Would I be condescending enough to enter and wait for him?

'Oh no,' I answered; 'never mind. Tell Mr. Cuthbertson I called.' But scarcely had I turned before my mind was changed. Swinging round with a suddenness that quite startled the boy, I told him that I had changed my mind, that I would stay till the master returned. The fellow looked at me in his sleepy Oriental way, but without more ado led me into the parlour.

The fact is, I had suddenly remembered the housekeeper, and I was not without some curiosity respecting her. It was no business of mine to pry into my friend's private affairs; but if fate threw the housekeeper in my way, who was I that I should resist the will of the gods?

It was a cheerless little room, I thought, though the sun streamed in from the sea, and the plum-blossoms filled the air with sweetness. The furniture was all good, but there was a half-Oriental tone about it which reminded one forcibly of the distance between the East and the West. There were few knick-knacks about; though here and there some exquisite *kakemonos* (scroll-paintings) showed up the incongruity of their surroundings. I saw none of the soft touches of the Western woman's hand. All was severely plain, cold, and comfortless. I could not help contrasting it with the rooms I had once known so well—poor little rooms with furniture none too new, but which the loving hands of mother and sisters had made so warm and homelike. There was nothing of home about this. Signs there were of easy circumstances: neatness was the order of the day; but not a chair nor a cushion was out of its place. Everything was prim, proper, and horribly clean.

Several minutes must have passed with me deep in reflection, and yet there was no sign

of Cuthbertson, or his housekeeper. Not a
sound was heard about the place. The boy,
I had no doubt, was lazily dozing somewhere;
the housekeeper, most probably, had gone on
a visit to her mother. If Cuthbertson had any
one else in the house, I was not aware of it.

At last, flattering myself that I had shown
exemplary patience, I rose, yawned, stretched
my limbs, and began to wander round the
apartment. True, Cuthbertson was a decent
enough sort of fellow, and in a way I was very
fond of him, but I was not inclined to waste
all the precious moments of my life in the
uncertain hope of beholding him. So, feeling
somewhat annoyed, I prepared myself a cigar,
seized my hat, and was about to sally forth,
when I heard the swish, swish of sandals on
the soft matting outside. Hastily slipping the
cigar in my pocket, I drew back against the
door, and presently in walked a little native
woman in a white kimono patterned with
broad leaves in red. Without appearing to
notice me, she toddled straight over to the
window, against which she rested, staring
dreamily out to sea.

For a few moments irresolution checked all

action, and then, with a slight cough, I made
my presence known. She uttered a little cry,
and confronted me with a look of considerable
alarm. The agitation flushing her face made
her look very pretty, and I began mentally to
congratulate Cuthbertson on the excellence of
his taste. Rumour had not belied her. She
was an extremely interesting housekeeper.

But my first endeavour was to quiet her
fears, and this I speedily accomplished by
keeping my distance and explaining the cause
of my visit. At first I thought she looked
incredulous, the native woman being ever suspicious of the European ; but when I explained
how the boy had shown me in, she smiled
faintly, said Mr. Cuthbertson was expected
every moment, and looked as though she very
much wished to relieve me of her presence.
This utter lack of vanity on her part affected
me to a singular degree. Nor was it wholly
without a certain influence on my immediate
decision. Here was I, at last, face to face
with the mysterious housekeeper ; and, knowing how little in this world is won by delicacy,
I was not inclined to flatter that excellent
superstition.

Undoubtedly Cuthbertson's taste was excellent. A finer girl he might have found with little difficulty, a greater beauty; but as a feminine combination she had not a few good points. Evidently a connoisseur of female beauty, the little he had had to do with women had taught him to look for the best. Indiscriminate admiration of the fair sex is a most commendable quality, but our admiration is for the man who can pick and choose—the man who holds his dignity as a thing of considerable value, his affection as an honour not lightly to be bestowed. Cuthbertson had kept himself aloof to some purpose.

At length I succeeded in quieting her fears, or, at least, in showing her that I had no violent designs on her plump person. I won't go so far as to say that my eyes did not attempt to sound her, shocking as the confession may seem; but the eyes, like all inflammable matter, are only dangerous when they touch. She, however, appeared capable of entertaining an inconceivable amount of modest eye-play, and after a while began to work her own slanting orbs in quite a coquettish manner. At all events, I imagined it as such, though, on the other hand, it may have been meant as a display of Oriental diffidence. The foreigner in his sublime self-consciousness is apt to shock the thinking native, and the dazzled eye may even take for encouragement that which was meant for a reproof.

Actions viewed in certain lights present a disagreeable appearance ; but if we twist about and get round to the other side, it is ten to one we begin to qualify and excuse. The facilities for falling are numerous ; the facilities for rising are few. But there is the mean course. Ah, well, the mean course never yet took any one to heaven.

I candidly admit my insincerity, leaving those who will take the trouble to think out the position to imagine what they like. I have only to record that when Cuthbertson entered the room he found his housekeeper and me making excellent progress.

I flush deeply at the recollection, but I flushed deeper as I saw him standing there in the doorway. The woman, who had been but a half-willing accomplice, sprang from my side with a little cry of alarm, and, clutching the back of a chair that stood near, hung her head

penitently. I turned to Cuthbertson with a
confused look and a half-smiling apology on
my lips; but the smile died from my face
and the flippancy from my tongue as I perceived the gravity of his countenance. Always
stern, he now seemed a very Daniel come to
judgment.

'Well,' said he with wonderful self-restraint,
'what does all this mean?'

I hadn't courage enough to say outright, so
I began to stammer some worthless excuse
which, no doubt, he rightly regarded as insolent
in the extreme.

'I understand,' said he, cutting short my
explanation with masterful gravity. 'Such
conduct is quite compatible with your notions
of honour. Friend and foe are alike equal
victims to your honourable scruples.'

I bowed, though inwardly writhing beneath
his censure. I felt that he was still the better
man of the two, and the feeling angered
me.

'Pooh,' I answered indifferently, 'we 're getting mighty moral in Japan in these days.'

'It's not so much a question of morals,' he
replied; 'a subject I should never think of

broaching with you—as it is one of mere black-guard honour.'

'Blackguard honour?'

'That honour of which blackguards unceasingly boast.'

'My dear fellow, if you will cage your pretty bird you must expect people to come and peep through the bars.'

A flush of real anger darkened his serious face, and I saw him press his lips tightly to keep in the hot words that bubbled to his tongue.

'Perhaps I had better explain,' he said quietly, his voice seemingly half-choked with emotion. 'That woman is my wife.'

'Yes,' I replied, affecting deep contrition. 'My dear Cuthbertson, I am quite ashamed of myself.'

I saw him shiver as though my words had fallen on him like a whip.

'You are mistaken,' he answered quickly. 'This woman is not my mistress.'

I saw the truth in his eyes, but it gave me such a shock that I could only gasp out, 'Married? You have married her?'

'I have.'

'Good God!'

'Why should you say that?'

'I beg your pardon. It is your own affair. I should like you to believe, though, that I never suspected this.'

He looked hard at me for a moment or two, and then said, 'Perhaps we were both a trifle hasty. One cannot always avoid a breach of good manners. But, if you don't mind, I should like you to give me an explanation of the look of horror that came into your face just now when you heard of my marriage.'

'It was a shock,' I answered feebly.

'Why should it be?'

'Really, Cuthbertson——'

'I should like to know. If you will pardon me saying so, you are a very tolerable representative of the world, and I should like to hear the world speak.'

'It has a harsh voice sometimes—a cold, hard, brutal voice. Pity it knows not, nor shame, nor truth—except when it censures the fallen.'

'And what does it say of me?' The man's anxiety stood out at every point, notwithstanding his seeming indifference.

D

'What if it were to say that you had ruined yourself?'

'I should reply that it was merely a matter of opinion.'

'But what if it is no matter of opinion? what if it is a terrible fact?'

He watched me steadily, his whole existence in his eyes. I saw his under-lip quiver in spite of his strenuous endeavours to keep calm.

'I think you overstate the case,' he said. 'Why should I not have married this woman?'

'Why not, indeed? All men are brothers.'

'I admit the prejudice,' he went on, totally ignoring my remark. 'We may degrade a thousand of these women, but we must not raise one. Raise, good God! Such is our Western morality here among these simple folks, these folks whom we hope to impress with our great principles. Yet if I disobey this law and do a just deed, I am to be punished for it?'

'Even unto the third and fourth generation. My dear Cuthbertson, the mere fact of your having kept this marriage secret tells its own tale. Prejudice, truly, nothing but prejudice. But do you know how strong this prejudice can be?'

'In short, a state of immorality is preferable to one of clean living?'

'Much, under certain conditions—if you wish to retain the favour of the world. It will forgive anything but a mistake.'

'And I have made a mistake?'

'Socially, you have dug your own grave.'

As he showed me to the door, he said, 'I cannot think you speak with authority. Why should society ban me for doing the right thing?'

'Society is never guilty of such a mistake; the difference is this: the right thing must be that of which society approves. Of course you no longer wish this affair to be kept secret?'

'No. I am sorry I have kept it secret for so long.'

We saw little of him after this; for once the marriage was known, the curse began to work. While he was supposed to have a pretty little Jap keeping house for him, he was a tolerable enough fellow in the eyes of those who couldn't afford such a luxury, and even the women spoke admiringly of that wicked Mr. Cuthbertson; but when it became known that that Jap was his wife all the interest in his doings evaporated. The fellows called him a fool, with sundry embellishments ; the women rarely breathed his name. He was passed in the street with a curt nod : oftener with averted face. The man who had been guilty of such a fearful mistake was utterly beyond the reach of mercy. Forgiveness might be almost stretched to bursting point, but discretion dared venture no further. The houses that knew him once, knew him no more. The decent fellow had sunk to the wretched outcast.

As for Cuthbertson, he bravely faced the music for a long time. There was a lot of quiet determination about the man, and, being wroth with the world, he bore its pettiness with a philosophic calm which was highly creditable. Manfully he set his face in the direction in which he believed his duty lay. In business, he was the same thoughtful, courteous man that he had always been : to all appearance he went his way in the same unobtrusive, methodical manner. In his eyes he had done an honourable thing in marrying this native woman ; and if the world could not see his act in the same light, so much the worse for the world. Had he been a swindling bankrupt, a ruthless destroyer of women's lives, false to his friends and his God, he would have found many to make smooth his descent : as he was only a fool who thought that what he was doing would be pleasing in the sight of heaven, he was quietly left to the care of the angels. When that happens to a man, he generally fares badly.

Cuthbertson was no exception to the rule. Since the day he found his wife in the arms of another, his confidence in her was shaken ; and though he may have had no just cause for suspecting her, his ignorance made his suspicions none the less acute. Then a son and heir was born to him, a little ugly, pig-eyed Jap which he could scarcely look upon without loathing. The wife's mother brought it to him with pride beaming in her eyes, for the advent of a son is a great event in Oriental families ; but he only waved her away with a curse. The hideous little monkey was no child of his—he would swear it on a thousand bibles ; and weeks passed before he could summon up courage enough even to look at it. When he did he saw the enormity of the crime he had committed.

From that time his life began its downward

course. A dangerous melancholy settled upon him; he was neglectful of his person, uncertain in business. When he was at home, he wore sandals and an old kimono; when he went abroad, he looked like a Japanese dressed in badly-fitting European clothes. His eyes, once so serious, grew furtive, wild, excited; the man who was once so sure of himself now stumbled and hesitated in a most painful manner. Then he got fits of melancholy, and for hours would sit with his head in his hands, moaning to himself, or gnashing his strong white teeth. Some said drink was the cause of it, but I think it was not all drink. There was a sadness in his eyes that drink could never claim.

Sometimes, they said, he had his moments of reaction. Then the degradation of his life would assail him with such vehemence that he would spring to his feet and cry pitifully that he was a white man, a white man, and that his place was beside the best white men in the land. While the frenzy lasted he was full of the noblest resolutions. He would retrieve the position he had lost; he who ruled once should rule again. They should kow-tow to him as in the days gone by.

Poor Cuthbertson! Those days never came. The frenzied resolutions were merely frenzied resolutions. In the midst of one of his noblest fits he saw his little half-breed child crawl in at the door and look steadfastly up at him with its ugly, pig eyes, those eyes which seemed to cry out mockingly, 'No, you are not a white man. You lost all right to that title when you degraded yourself. You are my father, and I am only a mongrel.' Then the man in him straightway withered; the bowed head sank beneath the trembling hands, and the desolate moan went up to the desolate sky, 'O God! O God!'

Gradually the ostracism became general. He lived as a native, dressed, spoke as one. Only at rare intervals was he seen. Then people told of a man with a bent back and rugged beard and hair who shuffled along in the dark murmuring drunkenly to himself. Indeed, most of us had almost forgotten that such a man as Cuthbertson had ever existed, when one morning some sampan men found his dead body floating in the sea, just off the English Hatoba.

EVERYBODY has heard how the *Pulo Condore* went down in the China Seas with two hundred and thirty souls aboard ; but everybody does not know how it happened. Oh yes, there were full particulars published in all the newspapers, and as a rule your newspaper is fairly accurate ; but in this instance it never guessed the true cause of the catastrophe, or, if it did, it very generously suppressed it. There was plenty of information about typhoons, those windy furies which are almost sure destruction to a certain class of ship ; there were thrilling accounts of the engineers striving heroically to stay the inrush of water to the engine-room, but striving vainly. Then came the vivid description of the helpless rolling in the trough of the sea and the inevitable foundering. Yes, the typhoon is a bad thing to meet, especially if you are deep-laden, or have to depend on

56

canvas; but on this occasion the typhoon was not primarily responsible for the loss of the *Pulo Condore*, though one was raging in the immediate vicinity at the time. She really struck on one of the Linchoten Group of the Loo Choo Islands during the gale.

How do we know? Well, all those who have not quite forgotten the incident may remember that of the entire passengers and crew only the second mate and two firemen were saved. The latter, of course, would know nothing of the navigation of the ship, but the second mate has been whispering some strange things among his friends; the rest of the story has been welded link by link.

The *Pulo Condore* was an iron screw-steamer of some three thousand tons register, and ran under the flag of the well-known 'Pulo Line,' which plies between the Chinese and Japanese ports. No smarter vessel of her class breasted those treacherous seas; nothing local could beat her in the matter of speed, and even the big mail-boats from Europe had to fire up to show her a clean pair of heels. That she was therefore a favourite on the route might go without saying, her long years of faithful service and her house-flag guaranteeing all that the ocean traveller cherishes.   As a consequence she rarely left either side without a fair complement of passengers.   To this fact may be set down the appalling loss of life.

Her commander was one Captain Richard Muirley, a name well known on the coast and thoroughly respected.   Not loved, perhaps, because Muirley was not a lovable man, being a somewhat gloomy, morose sort of fellow ; but he was a man in whose care the most nervous shipper would trust his most precious freight.   It was said that he knew every inch of the China Sea—every island, every sunken rock, every sandbank.   And as for typhoons, he had personally encountered more of those monsters than had any other dozen skippers lumped together.   A sallow, sullen-faced man into whose yellowy-black complexion the very atmosphere of the East had entered.   Stunted somewhat in growth, and thick with good living, he was not an attractive person.   Off his ship you might have taken him for a superior artisan : on the bridge, however, he was not quite so contemptible ; and once he looked almost great.   But that is to come.

As the rules of the company forbade the captain to take his wife with him, Muirley set his better-half up in a pretty little house on the Bluff at Yokohama, and there, every three weeks or so, though occasionally for longer periods, he managed to put in a few days. Then Mrs. Muirley used to go aboard nearly every day to lunch, and merry little afternoon teas were held in the captain's cabin; but they must have seemed long, lonely weeks to the wife while her husband was steaming south; and if in the society the settlement afforded she sought relaxation, who could blame her? It was what any young and pretty woman might be expected to do. And Mrs. Muirley was decidedly pretty—as fair as her husband was dark, as slender as he was thick. Indeed, some of the boldest of her admirers even went so far as to draw comparisons, and wonder: eventually she grew to wonder herself.

Muirley was not a society man, and his profession debarred him from ever aspiring to be one; but he could not with reason object to his wife's little social triumphs, though in his heart he may have viewed them with some slight misgiving. Still, they must have been long, dull weeks for her while he was away at sea; moreover, Yokohama was not a furiously fast place—at least, not in one sense. When he heard the first whispers of her popularity, he was not sure of the throb that sent his pulses forward with a giddy motion, but he afterwards convinced himself that it was one of pleasure. A man is always pleased to possess a fascinating wife. He knows how other men will envy him: he never seems to think of the danger of that envy.

Of all Mrs. Muirley's friends, male or female, the one her husband liked best was a certain Mr. Poynings, a well-to-do merchant in the settlement; and, singular as it may seem, Poynings often declared that Muirley was a man entirely after his own heart; and whenever the skipper was in port, the merchant invariably strolled round of an evening to smoke a cigar with him and retail the 'latest news. And there was no man who knew more of what was going on in social Yokohama than this same Mr. Poynings.

But unfortunately there were other retailers of news as well, and in the course of time it

came to the captain's ears that his friend
Poynings was rather more of a Lothario than
a man with a pretty wife should know, especially when that pretty wife has to be left alone
for weeks together.

It was strange, and of course absurd, but
the more Muirley thought of his position the
more unsatisfactory he found it. He half
admitted to himself that, perhaps, he was
hardly the man to charm a woman's heart:
no man can wholly admit such a thing.
Searching his conscience, he knew that he had
been good to her in his own rough way: he
did not quite comprehend the singular unat-
tractiveness of his style. He always felt their
parting keenly, though the knowledge that it
was only for a little while tempered its severity.
He admitted to the glow of pleasure which the
first glance of Fusi-Yama gave him as he came
up from the south. It would be folly to say
he had not thought of the risk he ran in
leaving his young wife so much alone; but
to think ill of one's own folk is the last
ignominy of the depraved mind; and whatever
Muirley's faults may have been, he had his
share of the sailor's generosity.

But faith does not necessarily mean blind-ness, and he began to doubt. Not that Poynings was not extremely circumspect ; not that Mrs. Muirley forgot herself for a moment. Indeed, that little lady was the pattern of what a charming wife should be ; but in a moment of sentimentality, after they had pledged each other in sundry whiskies-and-sodas, Poynings, growing confidential, assured Muirley that he thought that worthy mariner was the luckiest dog in the world ; and, upon the mariner pressing for an explanation, the merchant enumerated several blessings of which he was cognisant, among the chief of which was the captain's wife. Then the detective which is in us all here began a further probing and prying ; but try as he would, Muirley could get nothing more out of his friend. When they shook hands that night the merchant knew that his friend had altered.

Muirley must have thought that his wife needed a change very badly. At any rate he took her down to Hong-Kong with him, having, as a favour, obtained permission from the company. But, singular to relate, when Mr. Poynings knew that Mrs. Muirley was

going to Hong-Kong, he determined to pay
his long-deferred visit to that city ; and on the
morning that the *Pulo Condore* steamed out of
Yokohama Bay she had on board the very man
her master wished to leave behind.

The voyage down passed with little of
moment. Poynings was, perhaps, somewhat
attentive to the captain's wife, but it was the
attention of an old friend, and as such could
not, or should not, be misconstrued. Muirley
may not have liked it, being in the unenviable
state of doubting his best friend ; but there
was absolutely nothing in the acts of Poynings
to which he could reasonably take exception.
His wife was, if possible, more charming than
ever.

After a stay of five days in Hong-Kong, the
ship pointed her nose northwards once more,
having on board, among other passengers, Mrs.
Muirley and Mr. Poynings. Up to the last
moment the merchant had not thought it
possible that he would be able to get his
business through in time to enable him to
catch the ship, though he confessed that he
should strain every nerve to do so. The
captain, listening attentively, said nothing ;

but inwardly he prayed that Mr. Poynings might not catch the ship, that Mr. Poynings might never leave Hong-Kong, or that he might never see Japan again. Vain prayer, vain hope! Even as the *Pulo Condore* was preparing to slip her buoy, a sampan was seen hurriedly approaching, and, almost at the last moment, Mr. Poynings clambered aboard.

The rest had better be told in the words of the second officer :

'I had seen Mr. Poynings come tumbling aboard, and felt sorry for the captain. Of course we all knew what was going on ; in fact, the whole affair had been a subject of conversation among us during the voyage down. Some twitted the old man with not caring, and spoke of Mr. Poynings' great wealth ; one suggested this and another suggested that, but not one of them suggested that it was driving the old man mad. He was quiet, he did not interfere in any way : therefore he was callous. But I could see the change working in him, and I feared the explosion which I knew must come. When it did, it would be the bursting of no ordinary squib.

'Always a morose, sullen sort of fellow, his moroseness increased tenfold as we made our way north. He rarely spoke to a soul, and whenever he gave one of us officers an order, it was in a voice like the low growling of a bear. His eyes grew wild and bloodshot, and for hour after hour he glued himself up in the weather corner of the bridge, when for all the use he was he might just as well have been below enjoying a quiet snooze. But that was the strangest thing about him : I don't believe he slept at all during our journey northwards. I know that whenever I was about the decks, I saw him bobbing here and there like an old black cork on a stream, and the chief and the third had the same tale to tell. And all the while his face was growing more haggard, his eyes more fierce and gleaming. He ate little, but drank enormous quantities of brandy-and-soda, and smoked incessantly. But the curious thing was that he never appeared to get drunk, never even seemed in a state approaching drunkenness. Though, truth to tell, he spoke so little that it would be hard to say in what state he was.

E

'All the way up the Formosa Channel, the north-east monsoon blew furiously in our teeth, and time after time we had to slow down in the big sea. At this period the old man rarely left the bridge, but with his nose poking over the weather-screen stared steadily ahead. Sometimes I thought he was dreaming ; but whenever I ventured near him and his eyes met mine, I saw that the dreams he harboured were not of the most pleasant nature.

'Of Mrs. Muirley and Poynings I can say little from personal observation, as neither was seen much on deck during the bad weather ; but from what I heard I can gather that the old flirtation was going on in the old way, with, perhaps, a trifle more of recklessness, till at last it got so bad that the captain had to speak. It was the first time he had spoken to his wife of this thing which had caused him so many hours of excruciating agony, but she resented it so hotly that some exceedingly bitter words passed between them.

'That very night the burst-up came. It would, perhaps, be unfair to give any one of the versions which were flying about next morning ; but this much may be stated with safety.   The old man, visiting his wife's room in the early hours of the morning, surprised Mr. Poynings there ; and had it not been for the interposition of a couple of passengers from the next cabin, he would assuredly have killed the woman and her lover.

'He came up on the bridge just before I was relieved at eight bells, and asked me a lot of long, rambling questions—questions which bore little on my duties as a navigating officer ; and though I was forced to note the oddness of the man, not knowing the cause of that oddness I believed the long-expected had come at last, and that he was really mad. Nor was it till some four hours later that the mate told me the whole story.

'All that day he kept the bridge, taking his meals in the chart-room, or rather, I should say, having his meals brought there, for they were taken away again untouched.   He did nothing but smoke and drink, smoke and drink.   But there was the sickness of death in his pallid face, madness in his unsteady eyes.

'At six bells that afternoon we sighted the

Loo Choos, the gale still sweeping furiously down on us from the north-east; and when I came up on the bridge and found that we were making straight for them, my surprise was great indeed; for not once during my six voyages with him had Muirley steered any other course than the usual one through the Van Diemen Strait.   Still, there was no reason why he should not slip in among the islands if he liked, so I took up my position in the port corner of the bridge and watched. The old man was over on the starboard side. Now and again his voice reached me as he shouted, "port," "starboard," or "steady"; and when at last we got under the lee of a big island, which for a moment sheltered us from the horrible gale, he turned and beckoned me to him.

'As I drew near I saw the mad light gleaming in his eyes, and I could not stay the look of concern which rushed to mine.   He saw it and began to chuckle hideously.

'"This is what they call the Linchoten Group," he said, waving towards the islands; "a hell of a place for ships.   The *Golconda* went down here—on this point round the

corner." He stretched his hand towards a reef
which was now opening up about half a mile
off, over which the sea dashed and foamed in
horrible confusion. "Fifteen hundred people
went down in her, they say. God! what a
drowning! what a drowning! How many
should you think we have aboard of us?"

'"Between two hundred and thirty and two
hundred and forty," I answered.

'"Then we can give the *Golconda* hell?"

'"We certainly have a greater responsibility."

'He laughed brusquely as he turned away.

'"Did you say 'port,' sir?"

'We were now fast approaching the reef on
which the *Golconda* stranded. I could distinctly see the black, jagged rocks peeping up
through the white foam, and we were apparently rushing straight upon them.

'"No, I didn't," he answered sharply. "Are
you navigating this ship, or am I?"

'He laughed maliciously as he turned away
from me, while I, feeling rather snubbed, went
back to my corner. At all events, it was no
fault of mine. If he ran his ship ashore he
would have to answer for it.

'Nearer and nearer we approached the reef, and yet no sign from the old man. I watched him narrowly, anxiously, and, seeing that destruction was inevitable unless something were immediately done, I, throwing discipline and discretion to the gale, shouted excitedly to the quartermaster, "Port—hard a-port!"

'"No, no!" thundered the captain, "keep her as she is!" The breakers seemed almost under our bows as he spoke.

'"But, sir——" I began, our danger making me reckless of consequences.

'"Damn you!" he howled, shaking his fist in my face, "interfere with me, would you, you son of a——"

'The words died away on his lips, for at that moment the vessel struck hard on the outer edge of the reef. A look of devilish glee shot over the skipper's murky face. Then, turning to the man at the wheel, he said with a chuckle, "Now, quartermaster, you can port to hell if you like!"

'"My God!" I cried, seizing him by the shoulder in my excitement, "you have done this purposely?"

'He laughed a low, mad laugh of triumph as he shook me off, and springing towards the engine telegraph he signalled for the ship to go full speed astern.

'Of the confusion that followed I need not stay to tell. As usual, the ship had not boats enough to carry all those aboard. In a few moments we knew the worst. The water was pouring into the vessel fast: she was not expected to float many minutes. Two of the lifeboats were swung out, and after considerable manœuvring were set free well laden with passengers; but the seas were so high that neither of them survived many moments. And all this time the vessel was rapidly sinking by the head.

'The captain, leaving me in charge of the bridge, scrambled down the ladder and hurried away aft, and presently I saw him approaching, leading his wife by the hand. Mr. Poynings followed in the rear. Skilfully the old man picked his way along the crowded deck, pushing the clamouring people to right and left of him.

'" This way," I heard him say as he dragged his wife up the ladder; "this is the safest place in the ship. You will be quite secure here, quite secure." And he huddled her in behind the screen on the port side, though, as the ship was now rolling broadside on, the screen offered little protection. Poynings followed and took up his position beside her. He was very pale, but beyond that seemed as much at home as if on land.

'"See, the boats are putting off!" screamed the unhappy woman, her face ghastly with terror. "Why did you bring me here?"

'"Because I want you to see all the fun," roared her husband; "because I want you to see all that you are going to hell to answer for!"

'The woman hid her face in her hands and began to weep, but an angry look leapt to Poynings' eyes, and he clenched his teeth ominously.

'"You are mad, Muirley," he cried.

'"Yes, by God," bellowed the captain, "and it 's you who 've made me."

'"I will answer to you when and where you please," shouted the lover, the wind necessitating such a manner of speech. "But the last boat is almost ready to put off. Let her go. We two can fight it out."

' For answer the old man whipped a revolver out of his pocket. " If either of you moves, I shoot. Damn you ! " he shouted madly, his face growing black with hate, " do you think I 've done all this for nothing ? No, by God ! We all go to hell together ! " And as he stood there flourishing his pistol, he seemed more like a fiend than a man.

' The wife, burying her white face in her hands, fell on her knees before him ; and there, with the spray dashing over her hair, the ship sinking beneath her, and one and all face to face with death, she prayed piteously for forgiveness, the salt of her eyes mingling with the salt of the ocean. What she said may easily be guessed, though all I could catch was, " Dick, Dick ! " and, " Pardon, pardon ! "

' He leant forward and seized her roughly by the hand.

' " Yes, I 'll pardon you ! " he shouted, laughing hoarsely ; " let us see if God will ! " And with a shriller, fiercer outburst of mad laughter he pointed at the seething sea which was rapidly burying the ship. Then, looking round and seeing me, he beckoned me to him.

' " She 'll be under in a minute," he shouted.

"Run aft, lad, and jump. It's your only chance. You haven't a moment to lose."

'I was slow to act upon this advice, for I did not like leaving the woman to perish ; but knowing that the captain would shoot me without compunction if I offered to interfere —and, indeed, interference would now be useless—I slowly descended the ladder and made my way aft.

'A last look I caught of them as I mounted the rail preparatory to flinging myself overboard. Erect in one corner, pale but defiant, stood Poynings, fearing death neither at the hands of God nor man ; the woman still knelt, her face in her hands as though to shut out the view of death ; while the captain, with feet firmly planted and revolver in hand, stood watching them both. Then I leapt into the sea.

'When I had time to look about me, the *Pulo Condore* had disappeared.'

A NIGHT IN CANTON

FROM Hong-Kong we took the boat up to Canton, intending to do the sights of that salubrious city. Wills and I had long made up our minds to go and have a 'look see,' and it was mainly owing to a protracted cruise south, on which his ship had gone, that we had been obliged to defer the outing. True, I was not particularly intimate with him, having only met him in a promiscuous sort of way at the Hong-Kong Club; but as he was a junior lieutenant on board H.M.S. *Horrible*, he must necessarily be passed, though his 'bounder' qualities were as conspicuous as a church tower. Not that he was a 'bounder,' by any means, or a bad sort of fellow at heart; but he was a man of great stature and abnormal strength, which two qualities, coupled with a diabolical temper, made him a singularly unpleasant person to have any ill dealings with.

His bronzed, clean-shaven face looked as though it had been hewn out of brown granite by an amateur modeller ; but there were strength and resolution in its ugly outlines : the heavy, close-pressed brows were such as I should like to see in no enemy of mine.

We often used to laugh at such a fellow as Wills being only a junior lieutenant, for, if appearance went for anything, no post under that of admiral was big enough for him. Yet we feared greatly that all Wills's bigness lay in his big frame, and that his mind was lamentably out of proportion to his body. But this, while it could hardly have retarded his progress in the service, had no effect upon his geniality while ashore. Indeed, he was in every essential a capital fellow, when he wasn't drunk ; and, personally, I liked the blunt honesty of the man. There was a genuineness about it which, while it might set your fastidious nerves on edge, gave admittance to no doubt. He hated all subterfuge and double-dealing, all shams and pretence. He loathed 'side,' which in itself was quite enough to ruin his chances of promotion. He was one of those idiots who wouldn't wear gloves in winter though the marrow in his joints froze. I never saw him in a greatcoat. Nobody, I believe, ever saw him in one. He laughed at the idea of a sailor donning oilskins and a sou'-wester: he despised such fopperies and effeminacy. I verily believe that Wills will turn out a great hero one of these days, for he has all the utter disregard of consequences which is generally supposed to belong to the very brave and the very foolish. Death or glory was Wills's motto.

Well, he went into ecstasies over the first view of the city fragrant. He, with all the sailor-like anxiety to get his feet on dry land, had been pacing restlessly up and down the deck during the whole of the passage up the river; for, however much your landsman may rave of the ocean, only from a mariner can you get a proper appreciation of the land.

'Ah,' he cried, as we drew near, and the city slowly began to unfold itself, 'this is something like a place, old man! None of your cursed conventionality, little god-almighty admirals, or any other social iniquities. Hong-Kong is much too civilised, too damned respectable. Give me a place like this, Hugh, old chap,

where a man may enjoy himself without let or
hindrance.'

'Bah!' I answered, 'you don't know what
you're talking about.'

'Don't I?' he replied.   'You wait till I get
ashore.'

I looked at him inquiringly, but he only
winked roguishly, and then walked abaft the
funnel to light his pipe.   I waited patiently
till he came back, but he never condescended
to favour me with any further information.
There was, however, a leery look in his eye
which did not take my fancy.

I must confess I was a bit afraid of Wills.
It was not the first time, since I had left Hong-
Kong, that I had doubted the wisdom of
coming with him.   Free of the discipline of his
ship, he was like a lion loosed from its cage.
While things went well, and the beast was
unmolested, there was little danger; but once
the tail-twisting began, there would be a heavy
score to settle.   I knew Wills well enough for
that.   He was a royal bully, but without an
atom of fear.   As for consequences—I don't
believe his hot blood ever gave cool reason a
chance.   I had seen him wipe the floor with an

American skipper in the bar of the Hong-Kong Hotel, and though a dozen of the servants were called in to chuck him out, they did not seem to fancy the business well enough to attempt it.   Such a fellow should not have been left rusting on the China station.   Where England was giving and taking hard knocks—that is where Wills should have been.

As soon as we had made fast to the landing-stage, we procured an interpreter and a couple of chairs, each chair having four coolie bearers, and thus royally we set out to do a tour of the city, for there is no other mode of convey-ance, or at least we saw none.

Of course Wills led the attack.   Off he went in his easy-chair, a great pipe in his mouth, his face radiant.   This city of fetid smells, of filthy humanity, could not check his irre-pressible good-humour.   He was out for a holiday, and he meant to enjoy himself.   It was 'Hi, hi!' and a punch in the back if the pedestrian didn't get out of his way, or a gentle push on the tender loin with his Penang lawyer. Through countless narrow streets we went, where there was only room for one chair to go at a time : dark, squalid streets into which no ray of sunshine ever came, no breath of pure air : streets literally alive with streams of ugly, dirty Chinamen.

I think we saw all there was to be seen that day, which, when summed up, did not seem much, the spirit growing weary of the unbroken line of ugliness. But Wills expressed himself as satisfied, as having spent a delightful time, though I knew that in reality he was only living for the night to come so that we might set out to explore the notorious flower-boats. When questioned, he strenuously denied the soft suggestion. He was going to see them, of course; it was what every fellow did—but as for anything else—pooh, he never cared for Chinese women, ugly little brutes! Yet he seemed most sadly lacking in restraint, and had it not been for our guide he would have had us there at a most unreasonable hour.

But at length the darkness crawled in, and in due time we set out on what proved to be a prolonged and surprising adventure.

I was too unsophisticated to appreciate the peculiar manner in which the gilded youth or the *blasé* old age of Canton enjoys itself; while even my friend Wills. who dared not utter his

disappointment, showed it in the rough edges
of his grim face. In the dark, as I stumbled
over narrow bridges, it seemed to me that there
were endless streets of these boats, the smooth
water of the river being the roadway. Many
black looks were cast upon us as we crowded
in the doorway of these house-boats to gaze in
at the people, anxious to discover something of
exceptional interest ; but Wills at length proclaimed the whole business to be a ghastly
fraud, and questioned our guide somewhat
sharply as to his reason for bringing us to the
wretchedest lot of boats in Canton. The man
protested. The boats were the best in the
place, the ones all the gentlemen came to see ;
but he was afraid the people did not take
kindly to foreigners. He would have said
' barbarians,' had he dared, for thus uncivilly
does the Chinaman speak of the European.

Wills sputtered contemptuously, and looked
as though he would like to damage something
or somebody ; but at that moment, perceiving
a door partly open to admit a portly Chinaman,
he sprang forward, and, before those inside
could close the door again, he put forth his
foot. His shoulder did the rest. In he slipped,

F

I following at his heels; for, though I had no wish to force my objectionable presence upon a fastidious people, I had to stand by my companion no matter what came of it.

The portly chow, whom by his red button we at once knew to be a mandarin of the first rank, stood at the bottom of the steps and surveyed us with a look of contemptuous protest; but Wills, gracefully raising his hat, bade them all a cheery good-evening. To his salutation, however, was returned nothing but angry glances. Pretending not to notice these, he marched to the nearest table, sat down, and then calmly began to fill his pipe. Looking round upon the scowling assembly, he smiled sweetly and cried out to the women, who had ceased strumming their guitars at our entrance: 'Go on with the music, my dears. I haven't got any blasted scruples about melody.' Of course, no one understood a word of what he said; but his ugly, clever face was sparkling with good-humour and whisky, and even a Chinaman has eyes.

A curious scene; an unsafe one too, I felt. Imagine a spacious saloon with a profusion of gaudy gilding and carving; countless lights twinkling behind many-coloured glasses; em-

broidered silk hangings shielding little alcoves;
silk scrolls upon the walls with the wise words
of the philosophers written in gold (a quaint
conceit): the tinkling of guitars, the chatter of
voices, the close, sickly smell of opium mingled
with the disagreeable odour of Chinese cooking.
This is the scene we so suddenly entered upon—
so suddenly, in fact, that our guide was left on
the outside of the door.

The men who were reclining on the benches
drinking tea or playing cards looked up lazily
as we entered: the opium-smokers went on
with their smoking.   For them there was
nothing but dreams, and a vagueness infinite.
Here and there young girls with white, ghostly
faces and vermilion lips flitted, waiting on the
gilded youth, who seemed abnormally fond of
sweetmeats; or strummed the gay guitar.   All
was brightness, gaiety—and smells.

But as soon as we made our appearance at
the heels of the mandarin, and those assembled
saw by his looks that we had not come as his
guests, an ominous silence followed, a silence
most curious and profound.   It was as plain
as reason could make it that they resented
our intrusion.   I whispered as much to Wills,

and suggested a dignified retreat ; but I might as well have whispered to the north-east monsoon as it roars down the Formosa Channel. Not alone was he by nature a hard, obstinate fellow, never unwilling to fight, but he had reached a certain degree of recklessness for which state a certain fluid might be made mainly responsible. Under such conditions, I could only wait in fear and trembling, wondering what would come next.

In the meantime the mandarin had waddled to the far end of the saloon, and there, surrounded by the painted women and the *blasé* youth, he began to hold forth in a very excitable manner. Gesticulations were made in our direction, angry looks were flashed at us, and two or three of the more impetuous of the gilded coterie—flunkies to the last—came over to us, and with extremely threatening gestures began wildly to harangue us. Wills looked up benevolently and smiled approvingly, especially upon one little pale-faced fellow who, quite unnecessarily, had succeeded in working himself into a violent passion.

'You're quite right,' said Wills, though he did not understand a syllable of the excited

spluttering : 'you 're a damned good little chap
if you are a chow, and most assuredly deserve
a rise in life.' With that he arose, towering
over the little Chinaman, but still smiling
serenely, and catching the yellow man by his
neck, and where the seat of his pantaloons
ought to have been, he lifted him on to the
table amid the tea-cups. There was a furious
kicking of heels, a real smashing of china, and
then the little man stood high and dry on the
table. Wills immediately bobbed on his knees
and made the kowtow. This was too much for
the assembly, whose anger immediately gave
way to subdued titterings, and in one or two
instances to violent laughter. The Chinaman
is really a humorous dog despite his bilious
complexion, and you will turn him from his
evil thoughts in a moment if you can only
make him laugh—and keep him laughing.
That is the difficulty ; for he is a sly, treacherous
brute who unswervingly pursues his end with
a quiet stealthiness and enmity unexampled in
other races.

Wills never thought of this, or he might
have been more careful. But then, he was
never one to think, acting entirely on the im-

pulse of the moment.   Looking about him and
seeing the smiling faces, he strode over to
where the mandarin stood, and brought his
great hand down on that dignitary's shoulder
with a ' How do, old buck ? '

The portly official seemed to turn yellow
and white and green and purple all at once,
and had it not been for the assistance of those
who stood by he would have collapsed entirely.
The looks which he and his friends cast upon
the redoubtable Wills were such as to make me
wish that we had never entered the place ; but
my companion, oblivious of menacing looks,
went among the girls, paying them extravagant
compliments and chucking them under the chin
—a liberty which I am bound to say they
seemed to resent, for apparently even these
pariahs lose caste through contact with a
white man.

Wills kept calling loudly for tea and beer ;
but as neither was forthcoming, he somewhat
nonchalantly cleared a little table of half a
dozen cups of the former beverage, which cups
had duly been laid out for some one else.   Re-
freshed thus, he seized one of the native guitars,
struck some excruciating notes thereon, and

began to contort his ugly face into a series of
most undignified grimaces. Then, lifting up his
fog-horn of a voice, he bellowed a famous old
sailor chanty, the opening lines of which ran :

> 'Sally Brown, I love your daughter,
>   Heigh, ho, old and gone !
> Love her a darned sight better than I ought 'er—
>   Spend my money on Sally Brown.'

It was a most moving song, and Wills did
full justice to the fine sturdy verse and the
monotonous chant ; but how it affected his
hearers would be difficult to say. The girls
looked scared, the men little better ; while
each showed plainly that he thought the big
barbarian had gone mad. There was a
whispered consultation, and furtive glances
were cast towards the door. Then a look of
intense uncertainty superseded all, for Wills,
following up a glimpse of something he had
seen behind a curtain on his left, disappeared
in one of the alcoves I have already mentioned.
A minute or two of suspense followed, during
which I noted the visible darkening of the
mandarin's brow, the consternation of the
assembly : then there was a sudden rustling of
the curtain, followed by the scream of a woman.

The next moment a Chinese girl, evidently adorned for the sacrifice, bounded into our midst with Wills after her.

'Hold your infernal row, you little ass,' he was saying in a coaxing, endearing tone of voice. 'I'm not going to hurt you, silly cat. Chook, chook, chook! One would think the hussy had never seen a man before! Flower-boats are a fraud, Hugh, old chap. Give me respectable England. There, at any rate, girls don't cry out before they're hurt.'

The girl, in the meantime, her face white with terror, bounded over to the mandarin's side, and, resting her pale cheek on his capacious frontage, eyed the terrible Wills with a look of anxious curiosity.

'So she belongs to the old buck,' mused that worthy, favouring the official with a meaning look. 'Sly, fat old devil! I wonder if he'd explode if I hit him?'

'For heaven's sake, Wills, mind what you're doing! The fellow's a high official.'

'What if he is? To Satan with him and his high officialism! That's the only girl I've fancied to-night. My dear Hugh, this is de-cidedly hard.'

He began to look serious : I felt so.

'Let us get out of this,' I suggested, being a man of peace. 'The girl's a poor specimen anyway.'

'Humph!' said he, as he winked at the damsel and playfully called her a little ass. The mandarin, seeing the wink and the amorous look, scowled visibly. Wills, seeing the scowl, advanced still closer to that dignitary and patted him on the stomach.

'Easy, old buck,' he said ; and still continuing to stroke the stomach, he added in his best nautical voice, 'Belay, there! Avast heaving!'

One needed to be as reckless as Wills to enjoy the joke thoroughly. To me it seemed a joke of a very grim order : one that might land us in an awkward, not to say dangerous, position. Seeing the mandarin step back, his yellow, puffy face growing dark with anger, I once more implored my companion to desist, to come away ; but the anger, the disdain, which wreathed the Chinaman's countenance but inflamed Wills's resentment, and without more ado he poked his nose threateningly into the mandarin's face. That official, not liking the contact, spat ; and as Wills's ugly face happened to be in the line of fire, it was made receiver-general. He staggered back like one shot, and I shall never forget the 'Pah!' of disgust that escaped him. Then there was a sudden movement in the crowd : Wills darted forward ; there was a crash, and down went the portly official dragging his girl and two tables with him.

A moment or two of wild confusion ensued. There was a hurried righting of chairs and tables, a collecting of broken crockery, a frenzied babble of voices, and then the mandarin, his nose bleeding copiously, was presented to the view. Knowing we were in for it now, I held myself in readiness, for, however much I might have deplored Wills's behaviour, I could do nothing but stand by him in this extremity.

The mandarin, here sitting up, gasped out half a dozen furious words; there was a sudden rush for the door, but I, throwing myself before it, held the men in check.

'Good boy, Hugh,' said Wills, as calmly as a man might say, 'Well hit' at cricket. 'Don't let those beggars pass.'

'I have no wish to spend the night in a Chinese gaol.'

Wills turned away with a chuckle, and, addressing the prostrate official, said, ' Come, get up, old buck.   Fair's fair, you know.   You spat and I thumped, and so we 'd better cry quits.'

Speaking thus, he advanced as if to help his fallen adversary to his feet.   But the movement was evidently misunderstood, and in a flash a dozen ugly knives were bared.   Wills sprang back with an oath.

' So that's the game!' he cried.   ' Steady, Hugh, old man : these swine are showing their teeth.'

I saw it and called to him to join me, think-ing we might open the door quick enough to enable us to make a sudden exit ; but, as if understanding my words, three of the men crept round towards me and placed themselves be-tween me and him.   He saw the movement and smiled, but the smile was anything but a prepossessing one.

The situation had now reached a critical stage.   Fortified by the portly presence of the law, as represented in the mandarin, the bullies, sycophants, parasites, or whatever they were, showed a most threatening front, and I began to experience sundry curious qualms.   Under existing circumstances we might be murdered with impunity. Who would dare speak when the law itself was dumb? I saw the cruel blades, the sullen, ugly faces, and felt none too sure of the end of this night's work.

Presently Wills spoke to me, his voice as calm and indifferent as of old. Indeed, I had never heard it sound so free, so utterly devoid, of all trace of anxiety. He spoke without turning his head, his eyes riveted on the faces of those before him. By what he said I knew that he had at last begun seriously to consider the situation.

'I say, Hughie, old man, what armament have you?'

'A pair of fists.'

'And quite enough for any dozen chows. Do you think you can manage the door all right?'

'I think not.'

'There's no hurry, you know.'

'Impossible. They're only waiting a chance to strike.'

'Humph,' he muttered, 'how damned annoying!'

There was an ominous pause for a moment or two, and then, in reply to an exclamation of

the mandarin's, our assailants began a stealthy
advance.   By inches they moved—slowly,
steadily, and yet with a deadly precision ; hate
gleaming in their ugly eyes, their lips pallid
with excitement.   I looked at Wills and saw a
grim smile stealing down the corners of his iron
mouth.   Then, when I thought our assailants
were about to rush us, he stooped suddenly,
and the next moment he was brandishing one
of the heavy tables above his head.   Back fell
the Chinamen, their faces showing their fear
of this gigantic barbarian.   There was no mis-
taking the look in Wills's eyes.   Advancing
meant the scattering of somebody's brains.
Chattering with terror, the yellow men crowded
round the mandarin, who, however, never took
his hateful eyes from Wills's face.   The latter
addressed me without turning his head.

'Hughie, old man, come here.'

Profiting by his example, I whirled my stick
above my head and bounded to his side.

'These swine mean mischief,' he said, still
speaking without looking at me.   'I can see
it in that fat devil's face.   Just pop into that
recess behind and have a look see.'

'But you——'

'I'm all right.   Go, like a good fellow.'

There was no disputing with him when he took that tone, so, pulling back the curtain, I slipped into the alcove.   It was the same that Wills had entered, the one in which he had surprised the girl who had been the first cause of our present predicament.   It was a very small compartment, about the size of an ordinary ship's cabin.   On one side was a low bunk, the clothes of which, scattered here and there, showed excessive haste or great untidiness.   At the further end was a small spiral stair which evidently led to the deck.   These things, by the aid of a small lamp which swung above the bunk, I quickly noted, the stair in particular causing a thrill of exultation to sweep through me.   I noted, too, that there was a sliding door to the cabin.   The situation was not yet hopeless.

Though this examination takes some time to describe, it was accomplished with inconceivable rapidity, and I stealthily peeped out preparatory to entering the saloon once more. As I looked I saw that Wills had retreated some paces, and that the yellow men were dangerously near him.   Indeed, he was holding

the table before him now and using it as a
shield.   Even as I watched I saw one fellow
make a slash at him, and heard the blade ring
on the hard wood.

'It's all right, Wills,' I said, infusing a confidence into my voice which I was far from
feeling.   'Back gradually towards me, and
when I give the word slip in as quickly as you
can.'

'Right you are, Hughie, old man,' came the
cheery response.   'Ah, would you, you ——— ! '
and ring, ring came the steel on the iron legs
of the table.   But even as he spoke, even as
he threatened, he did not forget to retreat ; and
the yellow men, grasping his intention, set up
a furious howling and made a desperate rush
at him, but like lightning the table circled
through the air and went flying into the foremost group with a terrible crash.   There was
a sickening thud, a babel of shrieks and exe-
crations, and, taking advantage of the momentary confusion, Wills darted in beside me, while
I, with equal quickness, slammed-to the sliding
door.   And none too soon either.   The next
moment half a dozen knife-points were sticking
through the thin panel.

'Humph!' grunted Wills, 'where are we now, Hughie, old man?'

'In a devil of a hole,' I growled.

'In that case, my son, we'd better get out of it as quickly as we can.' And, even as he spoke, he darted up the spiral stair that led to the deck.

In the meantime the jabbering went on without, the blows upon the frail door increasing in vehemence. Two of the panels were already broken, and through the jagged apertures I could see the hideous black eyes glaring savagely upon me, could note the contortions of the ugly, pallid mouths. The door could not possibly hold for many seconds longer, and then——

I was startled by a crash overhead, and instantly guessed that my worst fears were realised. Our assailants had mounted the deck and had thus cut off our only means of retreat! But where was Wills, Wills the redoubtable? I turned inquiringly to the stair, and lo, there were his big feet descending! These were soon followed by the rest of him. His face was flushed, and he seemed to breathe rather stertorously. He threw a quick glance at the shattered door, and then turned to me.

'Up with you, Hughie, old man,' he cried. 'They'd locked the blasted hatch, but the way's clear now.'

'After you,' I said.

'Don't be a damned fool, Hughie.'

The horrid faces were peering in upon us: the frail door shook ominously beneath the blows. Without more ado I mounted the stairs, and as I did so I beheld Wills reach up, unhook the lamp, and then dash it through the aperture into the face of the enemy. A still more furious howl was raised, a howl of blinding pain, and with a crash the door fell in.

Emerging into the cool night air on the deck of the boat, I saw the cause of the crash which I had mistaken for the arrival of our enemies in the rear. Over the staircase, or companion-way, was a sort of hooded hatch, and this Wills had to break away to give us egress. When I saw the way the planks were forced, ripped, and torn as by an explosion, I ceased to wonder at the redness of his face.

But little time was given me for reflection, for scarcely had I sprung out upon the deck than Wills was beside me. Seizing the broken

G

hatch he, quick as thought, jammed it into the companion-way, and for a breathing space pursuit was checked. There was a spluttering and a howling below, but no immediate danger.

'Which way now?' I queried.

Wills took a quick, comprehensive glance about him, but the darkness baffled him as it had me. Before he could speak, however, a voice shouted out from the darkness, 'To the light, mass'r, to the light.'

'The guide!' ejaculated Wills, recognising the voice on the instant. 'But where the deuce does the right lead?'

'Let us find out.'

'Wise as ever, friend Hughie.'

We were about to descend, when the main door of the boat opened and out into the light streamed several of our assailants, the mandarin at their head; the other half was still sweating and cursing in the spiral way.

'There's nothing for it but the roofs,' said Wills. 'Follow me.'

Luckily the boats almost touched, so that we had no difficulty in leaping from one to the other; the only misfortune was that Wills leapt on to the skylight, and that I, following

so close upon his heels, deepened the catastrophe. There was a horrid noise of breaking
glass, a series of blood-curdling shrieks from the
people beneath, who must have thought that
the heavens had suddenly overwhelmed them
in their iniquity. I know I had considerable
difficulty in preventing myself from falling
through, and Wills's cursing assured me that
his long legs were hanging about him like a
reproach.

However, after much squeezing and cutting
of fingers, we managed to draw ourselves clear,
and, looking round, I saw that our original
assailants had succeeded in forcing the passage
of the companion-way, and were now preparing
to renew the pursuit; added to which this new
accident had brought another hornet's nest
about our ears.

'Onward, old man,' said Wills, 'and be more
careful.'

'Then perhaps I had better go first?' I
suggested.

A short laugh was all the answer he gave.

So away along the tops of the boats I went
with Wills at my heels, and a howling horde of
savages not many yards in the rear. It was a

breakneck journey, and we took it at a break-neck pace: a scramble here, a slip and a fall there, then up and away again, with an almost blind trust in Providence ; while behind us the crowd increased in numbers, and the savage cries of 'The barbarians, the barbarians—kill them, kill them !' rose thick upon the air.

Just then Wills began to pant and stumble, the reason of which I was to know later. Ex-cellent fighter as I knew him to be, he was but a poor man at running away. Seizing him just in time to prevent him falling between two boats, I hurriedly asked him what was the matter.

'I'm about done for,' he gasped. 'You go on and leave me.'

That was likely.

'Try,' I said. 'Better anything than to fall into the hands of these devils.'

As I spoke I helped him on to the next boat. Here, however, I found to my extreme consternation that the boats came to an end. Looking over the side, I saw the river flowing darkly. Behind, the cries of our pursuers re-sounded with tenfold vehemence. They evi-dently knew how the chase would end.

'Humph!' said Wills, in the old careless way, 'a corner, Hugh, old man. It's not a tea-party, my son ; but we must make——What's that ?'

Looking out across the water, I saw a boat rapidly approaching.

'A sampan, that's all.'

'Then once more follow me.'

Limping to his feet he dragged himself to the edge of the boat, took a look ahead, then another one behind, and the next moment he was splashing in the water.

'It's all right,' he yelled. 'Make for the sampan.'

There was not a moment to lose. Already the pursuers were close upon me. I could see their black forms flitting hither and thither ; could almost fancy I saw the hateful glitter of their eyes. Whatever lay before, there was infinite danger behind. As the foremost ruffian set his foot upon the boat, I sprang.

When I came to the surface I heard our pursuers' baffled cry of rage ring out harshly on the night, and I felt grateful for the intervening stretch of water. When I reached the sampan I found Wills already aboard. A splash, a scramble, and I was by his side, and, seizing an oar apiece, we soon shot out across the dark water.

How we made the old woman and her two boys understand that we wanted the Hong-Kong boat I never could tell. Perhaps they guessed as much. At any rate, in a very few minutes they brought us alongside, and once aboard I learnt that Wills, during his ascent of the spiral staircase, had been severely stabbed in the leg, which accounted for his inability to keep up with me.

No, I have not heard of him for a long time, but I don't think he has yet been made an admiral of the fleet.

WHY MRS. WETHERTON
WENT HOME

CAPTAIN WETHERTON was A.D.C. to the general commanding the forces at Hong-Kong, and was personally convinced that he was an individual of considerable importance. Indeed, he carried himself as though the whole honour and glory of the British Army lay upon his insignificant shoulders; nor, if one might judge by appearances, did he find the burden an exceedingly heavy one. Though small in stature, he atoned for this physical failing by an exceedingly colossal carriage. To see him swing along the road in his tight coat and tighter trousers was a truly awe-inspiring sight. The coolies kow-towed to him with apprehensive humility; flew from his path, not daring to use the same footway with him, and made their obeisance from the road. It is true he did occasionally acknowledge the

salutation, remembering that greater people
had frequently to appear civil ; but it was a
bit of a nuisance all the same—the penalty one
pays for greatness. It might be doubted that
greatness was worth it all.

Personally, Wetherton was a little dark-
haired man, with a dark face, a pair of piercing
eyes, a nose with a thick end and no bridge to
speak of, and a prodigious black moustache.
A formidable little man, to be sure, who, when
seated upon a horse, presented a front like that
of Mars. People used to say that he ought
never to be seen except on horseback. Mounted
upon his prancing steed, he was the perfect
picture of a furious fire-eater ; on foot he was
quite an insignificant little being, whom you
would think twice before you kicked, for fear of
hurting him. Yet he had a devil of a reputation, and had seen some fighting in the hills in
India. No stricter disciplinarian drew breath,
and while the men thought him a coxcomb
they knew he was not to be trifled with ; and
when they remembered that he had smelt real
powder—a long way off, perhaps—they frequently forgave him his idiosyncrasies.

And yet, when you came to ponder over it,

it was astonishing how much of the heroic that little body held. There was infinite resolution in the cut of his mouth, determination in his keen eye, while his snub nose completed the dogged, pugnacious look of the whole face. A pocket-martinet, that's what he was; a determined fighter every inch of him. One may be a giant without a giant's bulk; and Wellington and Wetherton both began with the same letter and ended with the same syllable.

Whenever he put in an appearance at the club, we invariably extracted a little quiet amusement from him, for his conversation, if at times somewhat patronising, was almost entertaining. There was a certain self-consciousness about the little man which lent a delightful flavour to his remarks; and while listening to him, you felt convinced that here was the man who could set the world in order, here was the man who should be ruling at the Horse Guards and not resting in a God-forsaken hole like China. But what would you? He could not expect the world to abandon its crooked ways for his especial benefit. Habit had become a second nature, and second natures come to stay. Wetherton, despite his martial yearnings,

was philosopher enough to see and understand :
but I will not go so far as to say that he never
chafed at the bit. We all admitted that he
would most probably do something if he ever
got the chance, for he possessed in abundance
those qualities which, on paper, make a great
soldier. Moreover, he possessed that best of
all qualities—a profound belief in himself ; and
the man who believes in himself can always
get other men to believe in him.

Then one day the rumour spread that his
wife was coming out to join him, and this lent
him a still greater importance. The news sent
our sluggish blood beating a throb or two
quicker, for we had all seen her portrait—he
had half a dozen of them in all shapes and
sizes in his diggings—and she had duly passed
our critical scrutiny. Of course we envied him
more than ever. Brilliant prospects, an un-
bounded belief in himself, and a fresh young
wife longing to throw herself into his arms.
In England a man does not fully appreciate
the manifold charms which surround him ; but
let him live long among the yellow or black
people, and he will go mad at the thought of a
bit of cool, white skin.

We were filled with a thousand wild conjectures. He had led us to believe that she was considered a great beauty in her native town—a renowned south-coast watering-place—and we began to wonder if she had any of the dash and 'go' of that famous resort. If so, some of us boys might expect a lively time, and Wetherton would have other than his military duties to look after.

As for him, the near approach of his wife brightened him up wonderfully. We had long known that the little man was inordinately proud of her, but we had no idea he was such a devoted husband. His face flushed and his eyes sparkled as he spoke of her, and we could see that, however much he was bound up in himself, he was none the less bound up in her. It was 'I must drop that sort of thing when my wife comes.' 'My wife always objected to this,' or 'My wife always objected to that.' 'I rather fancy she's a bit prudish, don't you know, and the life you chaps live here 'll give her a devil of a shock.' It was 'my wife this and my wife that,' till we began to wonder what monster of propriety was about to descend in our midst. And yet it was quite

pleasant to see little Wetherton cock-a-hoop—
not that such a state was unusual with him,
but his cock-a-hooping now was of the magnificent and enviable order. His martial face
relaxed its grimness as he spoke of her, and
even his fierce moustache took to itself a soft
curve of love. That he was superlatively happy
in the prospect of being united to her was
indubitable ; and little wonder, if, as he said,
she could give points to any woman in the
colony.

He had been with us now for more than a
year, and, though we knew he was married, we
had little hopes of seeing his wife ; for the
woman who can stay away from her husband
for so long a period is either very indifferent
to his personal attributes, or physically incap-
able of undertaking the long journey. The
latter, it seems, was the cause in this instance
and so accustomed had we grown to the
thought that Mrs. Wetherton was a hopeless
invalid, that the information that at last she
was coming out struck us as a sort of impossible rumour.

But, impossible as we deemed it, it was
nevertheless true, though the *Yang-tse*—the

ship she was on—seemed a long time coming.
Indeed, the first excitement was already dying
out when we heard that the vessel had arrived
at Singapore. This wakened us up a little ;
but being a slow craft, and having to face
a strong north-east monsoon, another week
elapsed before the *Yang-tse* steamed into the
harbour of Hong-Kong.

That night, after dinner, I looked Wetherton
up, curiosity playing the deuce with my discretion. I found him on the verandah pulling
thoughtfully at his moustache and watching
the smoke from his cigar pass into the mystical
shadows above. A young fellow was with
him whom I never remembered to have seen
before. As I approached, this individual very
politely rose, though Wetherton merely waved
his hand by way of greeting

'Welcome, my dear fellow,' he cried cheerily,
or with a heroic effort at cheeriness. 'Glad
you came round. Sit down and have a smoke.
Boy, another tumbler—quick ! By the way,
let me introduce you to Doctor Vine—the
doctor of the *Yang-tse*,' he added, by way of
explanation.

Doctor Vine, a tall, dark young man with

a long, loose figure and an uncertain smile, favoured me by dropping a long, limp hand into mine and telling me that he was extremely pleased to make my acquaintance, for which I expressed myself as duly grateful, slipping meanwhile into an easy-chair beside Wetherton.

'So the *Yang-tse* is in at last?' I said, as Wetherton took the tumbler from the boy and mixed me a whisky-and-soda.

'Yes,' he answered, but doubtfully.

'And Mrs. Wetherton has profited by the voyage?'

'Exceedingly, I should say. I have never seen her look better.'

I turned inquiringly to the doctor.

'Oh, we had a capital passage,' he explained. 'No bad weather worth speaking of till we left Singapore. I think Mrs. Wetherton is an excellent sailor.'

'She certainly looks remarkably well,' said her husband enthusiastically.

'One of the advantages of making friends with the doctor,' I suggested.

Wetherton looked meaningly at me, and, immediately conscious of having made a false

step, I grew confused. His shifty, piercing
eyes met mine. I saw his heavy brows contract, a rigid look steal down his face. Then
he fumbled his cigar into his mouth and
began to smoke violently. The doctor quietly
sipped his whisky-and-soda and lit a fresh
cigarette. I at once led the conversation into
another channel, and we were discussing the
benefits to be derived from the rainy season
in Hong-Kong when Mrs. Wetherton burst
upon the scene.

With reluctance I admit that the first view
of her did not fulfil expectations. Wetherton
had led us to believe that she was in every
essential a model of her sex, whereas her
figure was very slight, not to say thin, her
hips and chest apparently undeveloped, her
face absolutely colourless. At least, so it
appeared to me in the uncertain light. Fine
teeth she had, to be sure, and fine eyes, if
somewhat heavy. Indeed, such heavy eyes
seemed to be fixed wrongly in such a little
face. But they were expressive, ye gods!
And the light stealing through the loose
masses of her pale brown hair lit it with
gleams of fire. As she stood there in her

white dinner-dress I compared her with sprites innumerable, but never once with a woman of flesh and blood.

The hand she gave to me at parting was firm, if dry and cold, and this latter quality seemed to strengthen the strange opinion I had formed of her. Somehow I did not envy Wetherton the possession of his icicle, though there was some consolation in knowing that no icicle could stand the climate of Hong-Kong.

As I was going to walk back to the club, I asked the doctor if his course lay in a similar direction. He started nervously, looked at his watch, and said he feared it was getting rather late. Wetherton continued his strenuous puffing, but his wife exclaimed that it was ridiculously early, and begged I would not think of rushing away so soon. She wanted me to tell her more about the place, the people; what was the thing and what was not the thing, and answer a thousand other inconsequent queries. Of course I declared I was hers to command, but that she really must excuse me to-night, as I had a very important engagement. She pouted prettily, said she believed all the people in Hong-Kong were horrid, and then very graciously allowed me to depart.

The next morning I met her in the Queen's Road, and stood chatting with her for a minute or two before Lane-Crawford's. The doctor of the *Yang-tse* was her escort, and in the broad daylight he looked more like a second-rate clerk than ever. Nor did the daylight render her more fascinating. The mystic charm of the evening had flown, and a little pale-faced woman with drab hair stood before me. I went away feeling that Wetherton had been hugging a delusion to his soul, for which that arrant fraud, Distance, was mainly responsible. Who has not gloated over the irregular features of his dear till they become perfect in their classic cut ? Her undeveloped figure takes to itself a delightful contour : even her empty talk has a resounding fulness as of the sea.

I saw her again that night at a bazaar at the Town Hall. Wetherton was with her this time—that is, he was as near as he could get. The doctor's long figure had blotted him out, and a curious slouch the medico

H

looked in his long tails and black tie. He had evidently been dining with the Wethertons.

And thus it was all the time the *Yang-tse* was in port. Wherever you saw Mrs. Wetherton you had not far to look to catch a glimpse of the doctor, who seemed to follow her about like a great stupid dog.

Of course the fellows began to talk. First it was an extremely knowing look, then a smile, then an expression of good-will towards Wetherton. I like such expressions of good-will. They are so consoling. But people will talk in these small places, the curse of such places being that you cannot do a thing without your neighbours knowing it. Wetherton, however, being perfectly oblivious of their good-will, went unconcernedly on his way, and, if he had any qualms, he managed most skilfully to conceal them. His black moustachios still retained their formidable bristle; in fact, it might almost be said they bristled more than ever. To all outward appearance Mars himself had set the seal upon that face. And yet I thought that the eyes were not as steady as of yore.

I met him again some three days after the *Yang-tse* had sailed for Shanghai, and speedily learnt that the doctor had gone with her.

'Shanghai!' I echoed quite innocently, for at times the best of us are nothing better than sucking doves. 'I thought she had gone home.'

And then, before he knew what he was doing, he blurted out, 'I wish to God she had.'

He saw the surprise in my face, and flushed darkly. Then taking out his handkerchief and mopping his forehead, he bitterly complained of the excessive heat for that time of the year. Poor little chap!

Some two weeks later I met Mrs. Wetherton in her chair, and, behold! there was the long doctor walking by her side! So the *Yang-tse* had returned from the north! I passed on with a bow and the stereotyped smile, but I was not without the belief that there might be serious developments at any moment. The doctor, though stupid, had the tenacity of the mule; the woman, though frail of body, was not without some force of character. She would be very thin one day, angular and ugly, but she would nevertheless issue the word of

command.   Woe betide the underling who dis-
obeyed those clean-cut lips!

I only called once after the *Yang-tse* had
returned, but the reception I met with was one
not calculated to appease my personal vanity.
The doctor was there, Wetherton was there;
and while the former seemed exceptionally
stupid, the latter appeared like a man who
knows not whether to charge or to retreat.
Mrs. Wetherton was polite, if distant, but as
unsociable as a woman with a headache.
Indeed, she only seemed capable of the least
utterance after inhaling the inspiration from
her smelling-bottle.

Wetherton saw me to the gate, and at my
expression of the fear that his wife was not
looking well he launched out into a fierce
diatribe against the island.   It was not fit for
white men to live in, much less delicate white
women, and he was a fool ever to have allowed
his wife to come out.   She couldn't breathe,
simply couldn't breathe, in the heavy atmosphere, and—here he shook his head gravely—
he had no wish to leave her at Happy Valley,
pretty as that resting-place was.   Though I
didn't think such a contingency was possible,

I hypocritically told him to cheer up and hope for the best. The climate always affected new comers more or less, but it was marvellous how soon they grew accustomed to it. I knew it would rapidly improve once the *Yang-tse* left the harbour.

If I remember rightly, the ship stayed about a week in port on her homeward voyage ; and though I saw neither Mrs. Wetherton nor the doctor during that period, I heard that he was still as attentive as ever, and that Wetherton was rapidly developing into the worst-tempered man in Hong-Kong. The woman, I could believe, was cool enough. I could imagine her thin, curling lips, her white, placid face, her heavy eyes aglow with determination. Wetherton would find it much easier to rule five thousand able-bodied privates than one such delicate woman.

The night before he sailed, the doctor dined with the Wethertons at the Hong-Kong Hotel, and I afterwards saw them at the theatre, apparently enjoying the rather stale humours of a local Christy-minstrel show ; but as to what happened after there is considerable doubt. One says one thing, another tells you

a totally different story, and between con-
flicting rumours a pretty set of exaggerations
was circulated. But it is a fact, and one to
which the policeman on the landing-stage will
bear witness, that between half-past five and
six on the morning that the *Yang-tse* put to
sea, Captain Wetherton, his face livid with
excitement, his attire in a shocking state of
disorder, arrived and made some breathless
inquiries concerning that particular ship.

'Sampan!' he shouted wildly, 'sampan!' and
when the boat came alongside, he stepped
aboard, and, waving his hand out across the
bay, cried, 'The *Yang-tse*, quick, quick—the
Yang-tse!' The sampan man looked up with
open mouth and a smile peculiarly Chinese.

' *Yang-tse* 'ave all-ee same gone, Cap'n.'

Wetherton looked round like a man in a
dream, and clutched the roof of the sampan
for support.

'Is that so, constable?'

'Indeed, sir, yes. The *Yang-tse* sailed at
daybreak.'

Wetherton groped his way out of the boat,
and staggered across the road like a drunken
man.

When I met him a week after, I thought he had aged a good ten years. His head was not carried as proudly as of yore: even his tight trousers had lost their spruce, aggressive look.

'They tell me Mrs. Wetherton has gone home in the *Yang-tse*?' I inquired.

'Yes,' he said, with a bold attempt at easy familiarity; 'I was always afraid this damned climate would never suit her.'

OF course everybody laughed at the idea: everybody naturally would. Let a thing be ever so little beyond the comprehension of the ordinary mortal, and he is sure to jeer at it. The thing is right or wrong according to the way it appeals to him, or as fashion dictates. This thing appealed to his scepticism, and he laughed. He laughed rudely at the simple tale of the sampan men, who swore by the holy ashes of their ancestors that they had seen *it*; he smiled superciliously at the earnest narratives of the white sailors, who, while returning to their ships, had also seen *it*. Everybody knows the state a white sailor is in after he has spent a few hours ashore. Really, if better evidence were not forthcoming, it would be as well to dismiss the subject at once and for ever.

And yet the *thing* had been seen. Those who had thought it worth their while to investigate the matter were convinced that it was no lying talk of the Chinaman, no drunken fancy of the white sailor.   After all, those most intimately acquainted with sailors knew quite well that even among that benighted fraternity there were men who could go ashore and enjoy themselves rationally; while even the sailor drunk ashore is a different being from the sailor drunk aboard.   Stupid he may be, but he knows his way about a ship, and can tell you which way the wind's blowing. It was all hearsay, of course.   No commission of inquiry had sat upon the matter: there was no unassailable evidence.   It was merely a rumour which you might credit or discredit as you thought fit.

The rumour was this, and it arose among the sampan people who sleep on the boats, and who know everything that goes on in the harbour.   They said that on more than one occasion a phantom junk had been seen to steal through the Ly-ee-moon Pass, sail steadily down the Kowloon side, and disappear southwards through the Sulphur Channel.   But, as usual, the evidence was contradictory. Some said the phantom scudded along at a

terrific rate, leaving on the mind an impression
of a junk in full sail ; others said that the sails
only were luminous, while others again declared
that the sails were luminous only at intervals.
Out of such a web of contradiction who could
be expected to find the right thread ?   A
Chinese puzzle, indeed, over which the supercilious sneered, the unbeliever scoffed, and the
plodding star-gazer wondered.

For a long time no one but the sampan
people had any cognisance of the fact, if fact it
were ; and even many of them were known to
be incredulous : for, though absurdly childish
in many things, your Chinaman, being a natural
liar, is a true sceptic.   Yet so many had seen
the phantom, or had sworn they had, that to
disbelieve altogether in its existence was next
to impossible.   So the story gathered and
grew strong among them ; but being a people
apart, it was a long time before the rumour
reached the ears of the white population.
And then, as we have seen, it only came to
be laughed at.

The officials, naturally, were the last persons
to hear of it ; and when they did, the official lip
curled like the tongue of an ant-eater, and for

several months the Phantom Junk was tabooed.
No man likes to be thought an idiot, and to
mention that spectral craft, except by way of
ridicule, was to lay yourself open to considerable misapprehension.   But one night, or,
rather, early one morning, while the commander of H.M.S. *Awful* was being conveyed
to his ship, he saw, or thought he saw, the
spectral junk in the offing on the Kowloon side
of the Pass.   Of course, it was early in the
morning, when the light is uncertain, and he
had been at a merry meeting in a 'piecee
house allee same belong top-side'; but at the
same time the word of one of her Majesty's
officers is a sacred thing.   No one could
possibly accuse such a hero of being drunk;
no one would think of hinting that he could
possibly see double.   Of course the smile was
as supercilious as ever, but the commander of
the *Awful* was a man to be taken seriously.

It was marvellous how he stuck to his story.
They might argue and laugh and jeer till they
were sick, but he knew perfectly well that he
had seen something for which he could not
satisfactorily account, and that something was
the gleaming white sails of a junk.   For a

moment only they shone out, and, ere he could call the attention of his sampan coolies to the curious phenomenon, the thing had disappeared. He made the men lay on their oars and for a full quarter of an hour stand staring out in the darkness; but nothing coming of the scrutiny, he went aboard.

Now, when the Government officials heard that one of her Majesty's officers had actually seen this reprehensible phantom, they immediately began to move in the matter, and, after due deliberation, the police launch was ordered out to intercept the midnight voyager; but though, every night for a week, it hung around the entrance of the Ly-ee-moon Pass, nor left its post till the phantom-scaring day broke, it never caught sight nor sign of the spectre.

The officials naturally felt that they had been hoaxed. Of course they knew all along that there was no ghost, but they thought they might lay their hands on the rascals who had been scaring the lives out of the harbour-folk. As for the commander of the *Awful*—well, the less said about the state that gentleman was in the better. Responsible men who go about seeing phantom junks ought to be locked up.

But that worthy sea-dog was not to be laughed down. He stuck gallantly to his story in spite of sneers and jeers. They might say what they liked, but he would take his dying oath that he was perfectly sober on that memorable night, and that, being sober, and in full possession of what little reason God had given him (here he meant to be sarcastic), he had most certainly seen the luminous sails of a junk start, as it were, out of blackness, and almost as suddenly disappear again ; and they could take it or leave it, but it was the truth, nevertheless.

All this was put down to that magnificent obstinacy of the Briton, who never admits defeat, no matter how severe the drubbing : a consoling sort of idiosyncrasy, if at times a trifle absurd. But there happened to be one man among the officials who possessed a little more imagination than his hidebound brothers, and, in the face of official feeling, he let it be known that he believed implicitly in the statement of the commander of the *Awful*. He had not pursued the usual high official course and let his subordinates bring him a string of nonsensical tales to be swallowed without a knowledge of their composition ; but he had gone among the sampan men, carefully sifted their evidence, and eventually came to the conclusion that, phantom or no phantom, the tale told by the more intelligent of the watermen agreed in every particular with that of the commander of the *Awful.* A dozen different stories he heard, all told in a dozen different ways ; but the one which seemed most prevalent, and which boasted of the greatest number of adherents, was the one that told only of the luminous sails.

Now, when my friend came to me with his theory well developed, protesting against the supineness and meanness of the Government, who would not allow him to use the official launch, I immediately offered him the loan of mine, an offer at which he instantly jumped.

'My dear fellow,' he cried joyfully, 'it's just what I wanted, only I didn't like to ask. Give me a week, just one little week ; and if by then I haven't solved this mystery, I will admit to being baffled.'

Though somewhat sceptical myself, his enthusiasm gradually crept into my blood ; and when, later on, I offered to accompany him in his search for the Phantom Junk, he received the offer with every token of pleasure.

'And when shall it be?' I asked.

'We will start at eleven o'clock to-night.'

'Good.   I will be ready.'

'And, by the way,' he said, coming back and looking me meaningly in the eyes, 'you had better bring your revolver with you, for, unless I am much mistaken, we shall find these phantoms very human.'

A few minutes after eleven that night we slipped our moorings and stole quietly out towards the Pass, extinguishing our lights as soon as we had cleared the men-of-war. But though we cruised about in the darkness for a good four hours, we never caught the slightest glimpse of the Phantom Junk. The next night misfortune still attended us ; and a like disappointment awaited us on our third essay. My friend Kernot began to look anxious, and I began to laugh. Our spectre, though certainly a most perverse creature, would no doubt oblige us before the week ran out. Kernot did not take my pleasantries too good-naturedly. With him it was no laughing matter. He had almost pledged his professional reputation on the authenticity of the story, and that reputation was a considerable thing to him. So, though I could not refrain from having an occasional dig at the Phantom Junk, I tried to recollect what it meant to my friend, and curbed my allusions accordingly.

The sky was overcast and the rain threatened as we set out on our fourth attempt. Away across the water came the wind in savage gusts, a mournful howl seeming to tear itself out of the very bosom of the night. My flesh responded with an uncanny sort of shiver, and involuntarily I buttoned my pilot coat up round my throat. Our usual precautions were observed towards the war-ships, and not till we had them dead astern did we extinguish our lights. Then Kernot and I took up our positions well forward, the engines went slow, and the little launch crept out towards the sea.

We hugged the northern side of the Pass, thinking that in Kowloon way we might the more readily happen on the stranger; but, as usual, without success. The wind also began to blow more steadily, and when we turned for the open sea we met its full force. In an incredibly short space of time the sea rose, and as we shot along the mouth of the Pass we had a most unpleasant experience. Then began a slow roll back, for we had only to keep her straight; the tide which came swirling in did the rest.

As I now began to feel a bit nipped by the cold, I suggested a drop of grog. Pipes were strictly forbidden, and, like true heroes, we duly martyred ourselves; but grog was not. To my suggestion Kernot replied, 'Ay, ay, sir,' like the tar that he was, and I immediately dived below for some whisky. As I crept back, I made out his figure in the same position, but so absorbed seemed he in his look-out that he did not perceive my approach.

'Kernot, old man,' I said, 'grog!'

'H'sch!'

'What's the matter? Can you see anything?'

He did not reply for a moment. Then, taking the flask without looking, he said, 'I thought I saw something on the other side.'

'What was it like?'

'A white shadow passing over the sea.'

'Kernot, my dear fellow, you're dreaming.

I

Here, take a pull. You've got this beastly spectre on the brain.'

'Perhaps not quite so bad, old chap,' he laughed, 'though I admit its influence. Yet it was most singular,' he added, as if speaking to himself.

'The flash-light of some man-of-war,' I suggested. 'You can see the reflection a deuce of a way off.'

'Yes, I know; but this was not a bit like a flash-light. It was as though a lump of light was sailing——Ah, look—there—there!' I felt his hand tremble as he nervously clutched my arm.

Away on the other side of the channel, deep, it seemed, in Kowloon Bay, a curious misty light showed up. In a moment our glasses were on it, and we both uttered the same exclamation in the same breath:

'*The Phantom Junk!*'

Yes, there it was, with its phantom sails standing out boldly to the eye, just as the commander of the *Awful* had said. No other part of the ship could be seen, but we took it for granted that there was a phantom hull somewhere. For a clear space of five or six seconds the spectre showed up weirdly in the gloom, and then disappeared; swallowed up, apparently, by the sea or the black night that gave it birth.

The three men we had brought with us were fortunately fast asleep, but our steersman, who had seen the spectre, set up a horrible mutter-ing and moaning which proclaimed the extent of his terror.   Indeed, he even raised some feeble protest when he was given the order to port, which brought Kernot to his side with a bound.   There was a momentary scuffle, and then the chow fell in a heap on the deck, where he lay moaning incoherently.   With a quick movement of the wheel, Kernot brought the launch round, and, shouting to the engineer to go like hell, we dashed across the channel to the bay.

Making all due allowance for the pride of ownership, there wasn't a launch in Hong-Kong could beat mine for speed, and in a very few minutes I heard Kernot give the order to go slow.

'Do you see anything, Tom?' he shouted, for I was still keeping a sharp look-out well forward.

'No.'

'Can you make out the land?'

'No.'

'Damnation!'

'Port a bit.   I think I hear breakers.'

'We can't be as near as that.'

'Hist!   What's that to the leeward?'

I knew by the movement of the boat that he had starboarded again.   Indeed, in swinging round, we just escaped crashing into a sampan. For a moment only I saw it, and then it disappeared in the darkness.

'The dinghy of our spectre,' said Kernot. 'We must not lose him.'

I was not so sure that Kernot was right, though I deemed it highly probable.   At all events, if we could speak with the sampan, it might be to our advantage.

Kernot, who knew every inch of the water thereabouts, here gave the order full speed ahead, and in a moment we were flinging the waves to right and left of us in great style; but though we circled round and round, and in so doing lost some most valuable time, we saw no more of the spectre's dinghy.

'She has given us the slip,' said my companion ruefully. 'Now we must go in pursuit of the junk.' And without more ado he put the launch about, and back towards the town we tore at top speed.

'But, my dear Kernot,' I protested, as I joined him, 'if we can't lay our hands on the dinghy, how the deuce do you expect to collar the junk?'

'Of course,' he replied, 'this junk is no more a phantom than we are. It's a trick—a clever one, I admit, but still a trick. The reason? Well, there may be several reasons. I know of one very good one. We shall see if I am right. I only hope we manage to get through the harbour without observation. By the way, what's the time?'

'Ten past one.'

'A very safe hour. You know how the story goes? The Phantom Junk enters the harbour at the Ly-ee-moon Pass, creeps along the Kowloon side, and makes her exit through the Sulphur Channel. Well, we must reach the Channel before her.'

'She's got a good start.'

'True, but inside she'll have to hug the shore, and then she will lose the wind. I think we have a chance.'

The harbour was dotted with the riding-lights of ships, which, acting as beacons, allowed us to pursue our way in safety; and pretty soon we found ourselves steaming down mid-channel within measurable distance of our goal. Then, bit by bit, as the shipping in shore grew less, we approached the land; and under the shadow of it we steamed slowly forward.

Arriving just off Green Island, we stopped, and with our glasses searched the shadows opposite, but there was no sign of junk or any living thing. Then the mind, not being sure of itself, began to ask itself strange questions, and to receive strange responses from the sea. What were we doing out on this absurd adventure? Had we really seen the Phantom Junk, or had our imagination been playing tricks with us? To all of which the wind gave answer with a hollow, mocking laugh, while the spray flung itself derisively in our faces.

I know I began to feel a bit weary of the business, and was about to suggest that the Phantom Junk had most unconscionably given us the slip, when, without speaking, Kernot drew my attention to the island. At first I saw nothing, but presently a darker shadow crept out from the shadow of the land and pointed down the Channel. My companion put the wheel over, and like a snake we began to glide after the shadow, which, when it encountered the full force of the wind in mid-channel, made such a good running that we had to go at full speed to gain on it. But gain we certainly did, and with the aid of our glasses we presently saw that our shadow was a junk in full sail. Not a gleam of light could be seen on her. Like ourselves she was setting at defiance the port regulations.

'There's your ghost,' said Kernot mockingly, and yet with more excitement in his voice than he would care to admit. 'You'll see she'll turn round here by the Aberdeen Dock and signal to the people ashore.'

'Perhaps you're right,' I answered, 'but you're only going on supposition.'

'Anyway, Tom, send your steersman here, and, like a good fellow, go and rouse up those other three chaps.'

Having done this, he and I took up our positions in the forward part of the launch, and with glasses riveted upon the junk we watched her every movement; and, sure enough, she took the course Kernot had suggested, sweeping boldly down the little bay.   We, however, crept along in the shadow of the land, and, gaining rapidly on her, were well abreast of her before she reached the dock-gates.   Then with wonderful suddenness she put about.   We stopped also, and a few moments of suspense followed, moments in which I heard distinctly the hard breathing of my companion.   Then for a second the luminous white sails shone out: the next, everything was buried in gloom.

And now, what was to be the next move? I for one was uncertain whether to advance to the attack, or to wait and watch; though very little reflection convinced me of the wisdom of the latter course.   For, after all, what were we to attack?   What right had we to raid in-offensive junks on the mere supposition that they were—what?—phantoms?   My com-panion was evidently in the same quandary, though neither by word nor movement did he let me into the secret of his thoughts.   With glasses glued to his eyes he did nothing but watch the shadow opposite.

At length, after what seemed an interminable period of waiting, we distinctly, if faintly, heard the swish, swish of the long steering scull of a sampan as it was twisted through the water. I touched Kernot on the arm to let him know that I heard and understood.   Every second the swishing sounded nearer.

'There are two men at the scull,' he whispered.   'It is as I supposed.'

Well, the rest of the story is quickly told. Waiting till the sampan was hidden behind the junk, which we knew would concentrate the attention of the junk's crew to that side of their vessel, we advanced slowly out of the gloom and came up alongside the spectre just in time to catch her spectral crew handing out sundry cases of contraband opium.

Yes, they showed fight at first; but when they knew that the redoubtable Kernot was aboard them they succumbed with a perfectly angelic grace.   We towed them over to the dock-gates and made ourselves as comfortable as we could till day broke.   Then, when we examined our prize, we found that our phantom ship was a very ordinary junk, the sails of which had been smeared over with some

luminous compound.   A couple of ordinary
bull's-eye lanterns did the rest.   As for the
phantom crew, they were subsequently identi-
fied by the authorities as gentlemen who had
long been ' wanted.'

THE PASSENGER AFT

WE had only one passenger aft for Bangkok, and he was a Siamese who came scrambling aboard at the very moment of our weighing anchor. I was in charge of the gangway at the time, and to my inquiry as to his business he replied in very good English :

'This ship—*Amoy*—go Bangkok?'

'Yes. We are starting now.'

'Very good, Oyes, very good,' and he smiled complacently. Then turning to the sampan which still lay alongside, he beckoned to its occupants, and presently half a dozen of his countrymen came tumbling up on deck.

'Passengers?' I queried.

'Oyes, passengers, Oyes!' and he continued to smile upon me in the most absurd manner. I scowled, for I knew that oily Eastern smile, and the value one may attach to it.

'You've got your tickets?' I asked rather roughly.

'Oyes, tickets, Oyes,' and with another charming smile he produced them from an inner pocket of his blouse.

'Very good,' I said, handing them back to him after examination ; 'you go that way,' and I motioned for him to go aft : 'you chaps forward,' and I pointed the way for his body-guard, who salaamed and grinned, and seemed just as amiable as he was.

The captain at that moment leant over the end of the bridge and yelled out, 'Are you all clear there aft ?'

'All clear, sir.'

Then the engines began to throb, the screw ground the water white astern, and we slipped through the shipping with the ease and dignity of a tramp that knows its way.

The *Amoy* was only one of a well-known line of coasters. Sometimes our rivals called us the 'dust-carts of the China Seas,' some-times the 'scavengers'—it all depended on the mood they were in. At any rate, we were the very smallest of small fry. A mail-boat would not have condescended to signal us.

As our greatest speed only amounted to between eight and nine knots an hour, we had

plenty of time to settle down and get things
ship-shape before we reached the mouth of the
Menam.   Plenty of time, also, to look about
and give an eye to our Siamese passenger aft
and his six friends forward.   I admit I was
suspicious of him : of the manner of his coming
aboard ; of his secret, strange behaviour when
on board—a suspicion which his oily Oriental
smile failed to allay.   Then, as I tramped the
bridge during my watch, I often saw him
forward in close confab with his associates ;
and, once or twice, when unexpectedly approaching them, I thought they hid something
away in their sashes which they did not want
me to see.

That the fellows had come aboard for no
good I firmly believed; and this notwithstanding the fact that the captain, in some inexplicable manner, had almost taken a fancy to the
passenger aft.   Such an unheard-of thing as
the old man chumming in with a native was a
fact to be received with a certain amount of
incredulity, notwithstanding the assurance of
one's own eyes.   Mr. Wilkinson may have been
only a master mariner in a very humble way,
but he had a deep religious belief in the superi-

ority of the white man. To him all coloured men were niggers, and niggers, like other vermin, were best kept at a distance. He would no more have thought of associating with one than the master of a mail-boat would have thought of associating with him. The world is crammed full of gods of various degrees.

But there is one thing to which the white man will cringe as readily as his yellow brother —perhaps more readily; and that is—gold. That, like death, is the true leveller; perhaps the truer. We soon found out that the passenger aft was rather a person of consequence in his own country, and that the six men who had come aboard with him were his own servants or retainers. At least, such was the story, and such the old man evidently believed; but I had not yet rid myself of my suspicions, and therefore accepted the rumours in my own way. It had been my experience to receive some very ugly treatment from natives where I least expected it, and the recollection made me wary.

Not that I absolutely could convince myself that Chowfa—for that was the least outlandish part of his outlandish name—was really a bad egg. Only I mistrusted all Orientals on

principle; and even when he approached me
with his winning smile and his affable 'Oyes,
good day—good day, Oyes,' I regarded his
affability as an insidious yellow wile.   And
yet at times, despite myself, I could not help
wondering if I wronged the man.   He had
those horrid, soulless, Eastern eyes, which one
never seems able to penetrate ; those eyes
which have no depth, or, if they have, a depth
one sees not into.   How could one trust such
eyes ?   It would be flying in the face of reason,
the natural promptings of perception.   Yet, to
give him his due, he was most affable to me,
and seemed continually to put himself out of
the way to attract my attention.   He was
usually the first to greet me when I came on
deck ; when my watch was over he generally
met me near the companion-way with a
pleasant greeting and a good cigar.

In a way he admired me too—that is, he
admired in me a certain vastness of limb which
he did not possess.   Once he even went so far
as to seize my arm, and as I swung him off
rather roughly—for I was not fancying any
liberties just then—he smiled apologetically and
murmured, 'Oyes, plenty fight—plenty fight,

Oyes,' and something like a glow of excitement swept his dull face. I could not quite make him out. A fellow who looks pleased where another fellow would look angry is not to be trusted.

Though I had only been in the *Amoy* about six months, I was fortunate enough to find favour in the eyes of the captain, and more than once he had promised to make me his chief as soon as he could get rid of old Shiffles, who then occupied that exalted post. Of course I was deeply grateful, though I did not tell him that I had a different ambition from that of scavenging the China Seas. He meant well, the old man, and I ought to have been grateful.

The day before we got into Bangkok he came up on the bridge during my watch, and, after a good look round, beckoned for me to approach him.

'Seen anything, Wilton?'

'No, sir.'

'Um. He took out his pipe and began to fill it.

'What's she doing?' was his next question, which was one that struck me as being entirely superfluous.   If there was one person alive who could truly judge the rate of speed at which the *Amoy* travelled, it was her worthy skipper.

' Nearly ten, sir, I should say.'

' She 's got the tide with her ? '

' Undoubtedly.'

' Um,' said he, and bent to light his pipe.   A dozen serious puffs followed, and, the tobacco burning to his liking, he turned once more to me.

' Ever been in Bangkok ? '

' No, sir.'

' Um!   Queer place, queer doings.   Our friend aft is a Siamese.'

' So I understand.'

' A decent sort of chap, too,' said he somewhat emphatically.   ' I don't know that I ever took to a nigger before.   Just shows you, Wilton, what an absurd thing is prejudice.   Now, I 'll go bail that you 're not burdened with anything half so ridiculous.'

' No doubt I am much like other people.'

' Ah, that 's your dashed modesty,' he laughed. The old man was in a rare good-humour. ' You 're a very milk-and-water sort of chap, I don't think.'

K

Of course I blushed at this playful persiflage. The condescension of so great a man would have made any modest person blush. I said I hoped I had done nothing to lessen his good opinion of me.

'On the contrary, my lad,' he replied; 'and it's for that reason that I've come up here to have a chat with you now. I understand you and you understand me. It's a tricky business, though, and my respected chief officer's an ass. But I can trust you, Wilton,' he added mysteriously; 'you're as mum as the grave, eh?'

'I can keep a secret, sir, if that's what you mean.'

'Well, yes, it's something of that nature. You see, this Siamese chap, Chowfa, as he calls himself, is a bit of a pot in Bangkok; but by what I can make out he left that city rather hurriedly. No doubt for the good of his health. His version is that he was unfortunate enough to arouse the envy, or jealousy, of some one at court. He hints at a very high personage—king, or king's brother,—you pays your money. Well, this Johnnie, whoever he is, happened to take a fancy to Chowfa's girl, or wife, or something of that sort, and a fancy

with such a personage meant ultimate possession.   Chowfa tried to escape with her, but
failed, and so the other Johnnie got her.   Well,
that's nothing.   No doubt she liked the change.
But poor old Chowfa just escaped with his life.
Now he's coming back to try and carry her off.'

I confess to being a little taken aback at this
story.   It was so different from what I had
imagined.

'And what is your opinion of this story, sir?'

'Well, when I got as far as you have, I
thought it was a pack of dashed lies.   So do
you?'

I admitted as much.   Putting several things
together, I could not see the reasonableness
of it.

'But how does he propose to carry her off?'
I asked.

The captain withdrew his pipe from his
mouth and bent his head nearer mine.

'He wants us to help him.'

'Us?   How?'

'He offers me a good round sum—five
thousand dollars, in fact—if I will receive her
on my ship and take her back to Hong-
Kong.'

I laughed. 'It is not often that a good action meets with such a goodly recompense.'

'Now look here,' he said, 'none of your jeering. You know well enough what I risk.'

'But, sir, five thousand dollars!'

'Yes,' he muttered reflectively; 'I admit it 's a tidy lump.'

'And only for carrying a lady back to Hong-Kong! I would do it for half the money.'

'Dash you, Wilton,' he grumbled, 'I don't want any of your infernal nonsense. You know quite well that he 's not offering me five thousand dollars just to take her back. You see, there 's a bit more in it. The woman 's very strictly guarded, and you know how these Eastern Johnnies can guard a woman.'

'I understand. To earn this sum you must first set the woman free?'

The old man smiled approvingly.

'Or get some one who will do it for me,' he said. 'The dollars are all right. I 've handled them.'

Though I was sure I read the meaning of that insidious smile, I answered innocently enough, 'Surely no one would be better fitted for the task than Chowfa himself?'

'That's the awkward part of it. Chowfa
assures me that he is so well known in Bangkok
that he dare not set his foot ashore. But he
has half a dozen trusty men who know every
twist and turning of the city. If they could only
get some man of sense and courage to lead
them——' He stopped short, looking hard
at me.

'You mean, sir——?'

'I mean that there's a thousand dollars for
the man who can bring the girl off safely, and
I believe you are that man.'

I mumbled a modest thanks. It was extremely gratifying to know that I was so
greatly esteemed by my commander; but I
had no particular liking for such adventures.

'And if I don't bring her off safely?'

'Then you needn't bother about the dollars.'

'So there's danger?'

'Plenty.'

I thought his smile implied a reflection on
my courage. It was a curious, quizzing, half-
impertinent grin; a grin which said as plainly
as it could, 'Now, have you the courage for
this, or am I mistaken in you?' Being young,
I resented the suggestion. In those days I

had the courage and the daring for anything ;
though, as I said before, such adventures did
not appeal strongly to my imagination.   I
daresay I would have screwed up courage
enough to get my own girl out of a scrape, but
I wasn't going to bother about other fellows'.
And yet—here my practical good sense came
in—a thousand dollars was not to be sneezed
at by the second mate of a Chinese coaster who
was in receipt of the magnificent sum of thirty
dollars a month.   It was a temptation, and I
fell.

' I thought you wouldn't disappoint me,' said
the captain ; ' and, between you and me, Wilton,
I guess it 'll be worth more than a thousand
dollars to you if it comes off all right.   I don't
hide the fact that there is an " if " in the matter.
The chap who 's got the girl is a thundering
pot—quite a personage at court, so the passenger aft says.   It will be no easy matter, and
possibly may be a dangerous one.   However,
you 've got a head on your shoulders, and a
pair of big shoulders they are.   If one fails
you, the other ought to retrieve the loss.
Chowfa and his men will get the lay of the
land.   You, to avert suspicion, will take charge

of the boat.   We shall be here about ten days, but I don't think we shall require your services till the day before we start.'

The next morning we crossed the bar of the Menam and steamed slowly up to our anchorage, the passenger aft taking what seemed to me the most ridiculous precautions to avoid recognition.   But I suppose he knew his own business.   At any rate, it made me respect his rival.   His followers appeared as sailors, and the old man gave out that he had taken them on in the place of some who were leaving at Bangkok.   This was rather cunning of the captain, as it offered the fellows an excuse for staying aboard, and was to prove of use to me later on.

The men, however, left the ship as soon as it was dark, attired as ordinary coolies ; but they were all back again at daybreak, and had duly reported to their master, who in turn bore his report to the captain, through whom it reached me.   The men, as I guessed, had been spying, and would continue to do so till the time was ripe for a forward movement.

Chowfa, all this time, clung to the ship like a barnacle, never by any chance showing him-

self on deck while any strangers were aboard.
Sometimes he joined me of an evening on deck
after the work was done, and we had a smoke
together.   Then he would try to tell me in his
broken English how deeply grateful he was to
me, and with his soft, buttery ways would work
so on my feelings that I invariably promised
to do all that a bold Briton could to rescue
his beloved.   Poor chap! When you come to
think of it, it is a bit hard to have your girl
carried off in such an arbitrary manner.   Seeing the resentment in my eyes, he would give
my shoulder an admiring pat, or my arm, which
would have made three of his, a loving squeeze,
and murmur, 'Oyes, plenty fight—plenty fight,
Oyes.'   He also conveyed to me the desire
that, should I come in personal contact with
Kha, which was the name of the villain who retained Chowfa's treasure, I would summarily
flatten him.   All of which I faithfully promised.

We had been quietly lying at the buoys about
a week, when one morning the captain told me
to get out one of our after boats, which I had
no sooner done than he advanced and informed
me that he wished to give his new men a little
boat-practice.   Indeed, I was not surprised

when, on looking over the stern, I perceived one of Chowfa's men already in the boat. Chowfa himself was on deck, and at a word from him the boat was hauled round to the gangway. Then, as at a given signal, four or five men slipped down into it. It is needless to add that they were Chowfa's men.

'This being a ship's boat, and in charge of a ship's officer, it is not likely to be questioned,' said the old man, coming out on the gangway to me; 'but, to save appearances, you might purchase provisions of some sort. For the rest, you may safely leave yourself in the hands of these fellows. They'll show you the road to the bird's cage.'

I smiled, and descending entered the boat; the men in the bows pushed off, the others got out their oars, and away we went. The stream flowed pretty hard just then, for the flood-water had not yet run off; but my men laid to with a will, plainly showing that they were no novices at the game. So much, at any rate, was satisfactory. If it came to a keen pursuit they were equal to a ding-dong struggle.

Up the stream we went for about two miles, till the man in the bows pointed out an opening on my right, which looked like the entrance to a creek or canal. I immediately turned into it, and presently a landing-stage and several sampans opened up, the occupants of the latter favouring us with but an informal stare as we passed. I brought our boat in against the stage and stepped ashore, the man in the bows following me.

'Are you coming with me?' I asked.

'Yes, mas'r.'

The other fellows had already dropped down a boat's-length or two. I nodded approval. Then my companion and I set out, he walking a dozen yards or so astern of me, but coming forward to direct me whenever we came to a turning. In this way we steered an intricate course for about half a mile, at the end of which we ran foul of a high stone wall, round the inside of which several fairly large trees grew. Here my companion advanced smiling.

'Is this the place?'

'Yes, mas'r.'

'Um!' I looked puzzled, for I could not see how we were to enter through the solid mass of mud and stone.

The man saw the look in my face, and

pointed up to the tree. I could see nothing there, but presently he undid the sash from his waist, and made a pretence of throwing it over one of the boughs. Catching the gleam of understanding in my eye, he smiled and motioned for me to follow him, which I did round the wall for about two hundred paces. Here he stopped against a low gate, shook it and smiled. His meaning was obvious. He would mount the wall by the aid of the tree, then creep round and open the gate for me to enter. Very fine arrangement, thought I : I only hope it will be as easy as it looks. I then retraced my steps, and succeeded in reaching the boat without the aid of my guide. So far so good. I did not forget to make some purchases on the way back.

Of course the captain was eager for my report, and when he heard all that I had to say he confessed that I had a soft thing on, and that it would be the easiest thousand dollars I had ever earned. I thought likewise of those five thousand dollars, and how much easier their earning would be for him. I, however, expressed much doubt concerning the easiness of my task, more particularly mentioning the trouble I would have to find the woman even though I gained admittance to the grounds.

'I wondered if you'd think of that,' he said, 'or if you'd go blindly at it in sailor-man fashion. My dear fellow, you'll be led direct to the lady. The man who acted as guide was once a servant of Kha's. He knows every twist and turning of the blessed house from top to bottom.'

I felt relieved. Certainly the difficulties seemed chiefly to consist of the vapours of my own imagination. Perhaps the skipper was as near his five thousand dollars as he hoped.

Every day after this I took the boat up to the same landing-stage, and went ashore, returning with provisions of some sort, till our coming and going evoked no sign of interest from the lethargic sampan people.

And so gradually the time grew near for the great attempt, and one day, just before breakfast, the captain approached me with a serious face.

'We shall drop down the stream at five this afternoon,' he said, 'so you must make the attempt to-night. We shall clear the bar before dusk and apparently sail away south.

So we shall ; but in the dark we will feel our way back and lie-to within half a dozen miles of the bar. If your adventure succeeds and you pass the forts safely, give us a flare at your discretion, and we will answer it. We shall wait for you till daybreak.'

There was nothing more to be said. If daybreak did not find me somewhere off the mouth of the Menam, it would probably be because I was at the bottom of that stream. However, I meant to leave as little to chance as possible, so I armed myself with a six-chambered revolver and a dozen extra cartridges, and saw that my men were similarly equipped : indeed, their equipment was more complete than mine, for, in addition to his revolver, each man carried a long sheath-knife not unlike a Malay creese. I also had some provisions stowed away in the after part of the boat, likewise a fair-sized keg of water, thinking it just as well to be prepared for any contingency. I also took a dress similar to that which my men wore, and pigment to darken my skin, though, truth to tell, the sun had done that well enough.

Shortly after two bells, or five o'clock, I

intimated to the old man that I was ready, and we walked together towards the gangway, he imploring me to refrain from all rashness, and be sure not to use force unless absolutely necessary. I don't know what he took me for, but I assured him that I hoped with all my heart I should meet with no opposition, and I meant it. For, now that the important moment had come, I experienced some anxiety concerning the business—chiefly, I think, through the extreme vagueness of my plans. Imagination and distance had lent a certain glamour to the project; but now that the eventful hour had really come, reflection added the most unpleasing reminder that I was rushing somewhat blindly and foolishly upon the unknown. But it was too late now. If stupidity had its proverbial luck, all might be well: if not, we should be in a deuce of a corner.

Chowfa was by the engine-room skylight, talking seriously to his head man, the fellow who had been my guide; and as the captain and I approached, the fellow with a low salaam skipped from his master's side and descended the gangway, I following him a few moments later.

'Take care of yourself, Wilton,' whispered the captain, 'and for God's sake don't hurt any one if you can help it.'

I shook my head. Was it likely? I only hoped that no one would hurt me.

'Remember,' he continued, 'we shall hang outside the entrance till daybreak. Good luck to you.'

'Thank you, sir.'

I ran down the gangway and pushed off. A last glance at the old packet as my men bent to their oars revealed the red, excited face of the skipper, and the thoughtful yellow face of Chowfa. Forward the mate was cursing lustily among the men, but, looking over the side, he waved his big hairy hand. Somehow I wondered if I should ever see him again.

The voyage up the stream was accomplished satisfactorily, and the landing duly effected. Then, having to kill time the best way I could, I took my guide with me and rambled through the city, cautioning the men on no account to leave the boat,—a caution which I had good reason to believe they implicitly obeyed; for, returning after dark, and hailing the boat, I found them at their post. Then I put off into the stream and donned my native dress, and added the dark pigment to my already dark skin, the result of which left me a tolerable Siamese, albeit my bulk was considerably out of proportion to my assumed nationality.

Pulling back to the landing-stage, my guide and I quickly stepped ashore, and made off in the darkness, two more of my men following at a discreet distance. The three others were left in charge of the boat with the injunction to be ready at a moment's notice.

The night was clear, if dark, and not the one I should have chosen for our adventure had choice been given me ; but it would probably be some two or three hours before the moon rose, before which time I hoped to have accomplished my purpose.

In the meantime my companion and I walked swiftly and silently on, the few people we met taking no more notice of us than if we were what we seemed. Consequently we reached our destination without let or hindrance. Here, crouching beneath the big wall, in the shadow of the trees, we waited till our two followers approached. Then my guide, speaking in a low undertone, sent one to the right and one to the left of us, at which piece of precaution I duly nodded approval. The fellow's eyes fairly blazed with excitement. Whether it was with joy at thought of serving the new master, or paying off a grudge against the old, I could not say ; but, knowing something of his story, I may have had my suspicions.

But meanwhile he was nervously unwinding a rope which he had secreted about his waist, and which I guessed to be some six or seven fathoms long. He grinned and gibbered and carried on rather idiotically during this operation; but, though intensely excited, he evidently had his wits about him, and, by the triumphant flashes he turned on me, those wits were conjuring up a singular series of pictures.

To the end of the line was attached a little bag of sand weighing about two pounds ; and, as I took this up to examine it, the fellow grinned hideously, pointed up into the tree, and swung his arm. I understood the pantomime, and duly admired the ingenuity. Nothing had been forgotten, and I was quite willing to credit all the old man had said about the girl having been prepared for our coming. Had she not been, I foresaw no end of complications.

L

Just then my guide stepped back, and swinging the bag once, twice, three times, he launched it into space. There was a rustling of leaves overhead as the missile forced its way through the foliage ; then, hand over hand, he began to pay out the line till presently the little bag floated on a level with our faces. To seize it, to test the position, was the work of a moment ; but he had neither misjudged his aim nor the strength of the bough. Then, with another frightened, diabolical grin on his ugly face, he seized the line and went up it hand over hand like a monkey. I watched him till he was lost in the foliage, but I knew by the cracking overhead that he had reached his perch safely, and was making his way along the bough. He would, of course, descend on the inside by the trunk of the tree.

After waiting till I knew he had safely negotiated the aforesaid bough, I hauled on the free end of the line, and pulled it over ; then, coiling it up, carried it with me to the gate, not wishing any chance passer-by to stumble on it unawares. The gate reached, I laid the line beside it, and anxiously awaited further developments.

For a long time—several minutes it seemed
to me, though possibly it was not that—no
sound came to tell me that my friend on the
other side was moving.   My anxiety increased
by leaps and bounds, and I was just picturing
him falling an easy prey to the watchful Kha,
when I heard a gentle attempt on the gate.
So gentle was it that any one passing, who
had no cause for suspicion, would not have
noticed it.   I scratched gently by way of an
answer, but, to my surprise, he did not reply.
Indeed, for a full minute no sound whatever
came from the other side.   Then suddenly
some hurried work began, the gate was quickly
opened, and I pulled in.

'You've been a devil of a time,' I growled.

'Oyes, mas'r—plenty care, mas'r.'

'Why didn't you open the gate at first?'

He pulled my ear down to him and whispered, 'Kha's people watch alongside gate.
Expect some one.'

I could not restrain a sudden gasp.   Phew!
It was a close shave.   How close I did not tell
him, for he was almost fainting as it was.

Closing the gate noiselessly, he seized me by
the hand, and dragged me into an adjacent

shrubbery by the wall, where I deposited the coil of rope, and there we stood for a good three minutes anxiously straining our eyes and ears. But, no sound of an unusual nature reaching us, we were forced to the conclusion that the watcher, whoever he was, or for what reason he had been there, had surely betaken himself within doors.

Motioning for me to follow, my guide, who seemed to know every inch of the ground, skirted the wall for some hundred yards or so, and then bore straight across to the house, seeking the shadow of every shrub and tree that lay in his way. In this manner, and by means of persistent dodging, waiting, and listening, we advanced well up to the house, in the shadow of which we rested a while, to still our nerves, I think, almost as much as to gain our breath.

A low verandah, over which grew a profusion of rose-scented creeper, seemed to surround the house. By the occasional tinkling of a guitar, and the low laughter of women which now and again came rippling out through the open window, I guessed, and not untruly, that this building was the worthy Kha's seraglio. Here

it was, according to arrangement, that we were
to meet the beautiful Pakna, the well-beloved
of Chowfa, who was too great a lord to risk his
skin for the sake of his adored one.

My guide, who seemed uncommonly nervous,
and who had not yet got over the fright of
seeing a man at the gate, evidently wished to
find out for certain where the man had gone.
Therefore, warning me with uplifted hand to
keep still, he started from my side, and disappeared as noiselessly as a shadow.

For a long time I stood there, scarcely daring
to breathe ; but as there was no sign of him
returning, and as my patience was fast getting
exhausted, I decided to do a little exploring
on my own account.   Full of that intent, I
parted the creepers on my left, and was about
to step on to the verandah, when from an open
window opposite I saw a dark form emerge.
Immediately drawing back, I held my breath
and watched, but whether the form belonged
to a man or a woman I could not say.   However, I was soon assured, for, after standing at
the window some little time, the figure turned
away with a sigh.   I remembered all.   She
had been warned : she was waiting.   Her

deep sigh denoted intense disappointment. At least, such was the way I read it, and I acted accordingly.

'Hist!'

It was low, soft, but clear as a bell, and was done almost involuntarily. I confess to a few extra heart-beats just then. Would my imprudence ruin me?

Luck was looking my way for once. She stopped, peered irresolutely forward, and then advanced a step.

'Pakna!' I whispered, in a tone as sweet as Chowfa himself could use.

Again she sighed, and this time stretched towards me, muttering something in the native tongue. Guessing that she asked who I was, I replied in the same voice, 'Chowfa.'

This name made an extraordinary impression upon her, and, hesitating no longer, she advanced to where I was hiding. I immediately parted the creeper and stepped on to the verandah beside her. She retreated with a little cry of alarm. To reassure her I repeated 'Chowfa, Chowfa,' and by sundry gesticulations gave her to understand that I had come to convey her to her lord. Luckily, at that moment my guide advanced, and, seeing us together, he fell on his knees before her and bowed his head in the dust. Then she said something in a soft, low voice, and he arose, still salaaming as he did so.

'She understand, mas'r,' he whispered. 'Plenty ready—minute.'

The woman retreated back through the window: we slunk again into the shrubbery and there anxiously awaited her reappearance.

She seemed an unconscionable time in coming, and I began inwardly to fume. We might easily have been half-way to the boat by now but for her cursed dilatoriness. What the deuce did she want to go back for when I was there and everything ready for her escape? Her few trumpery trinkets, I guessed, which was so like a woman, and which would probably prove her ruin. It is always the same. No matter how near to foundering the ship may be, there is always some madman who stays to dress, some miser who rushes below to seize his little hoard—and goes down with the ship.

My impatience was gradually giving way to a generous rage, when she again appeared upon

the scene. This time she bore a considerable
bundle in her hand, proving the truth of my
surmise. Feeling extremely ungracious, I
again stepped on to the verandah and ex-
tended my hand for the bundle, when all of
a sudden a heavy footfall sounded on the
path not a dozen yards away. With a half-
stifled cry of alarm the woman instantly seized
my hand and drew me through the window
into the house. My guide, whose head only
had poked through the creeper, withdrew at
once.

The room was quite dark, but, as she still
held my hand and guided me, the darkness
was no great inconvenience. She led me
swiftly right across the room till I felt a
curtain brush against my face—the curtain, I
guessed, which partitioned off an inner chamber. Here she stopped, and we involuntarily
turned together. Looking backward, the open
window was distinctly to be seen, and further
on, in the dim light, the dark shadow of the
creepers. But these are only such things as
come to thought afterwards: then we heard
only the footsteps, which were now upon the
verandah; saw, in imagination, nothing but the

owner thereof. Then, like an apparition, his form suddenly blocked up the entrance.

I felt her little hand tremble, but pressed it reassuringly, and, terrified as she was, she gave me an answering pressure.

But in the meantime the man, speaking sharply, like one who is accustomed to command, stepped into the room ; but apparently liking not the darkness, and receiving no answer, he as quickly skipped back to the window, from which position he spoke again in a louder, shriller key. There was a note of excitement, of suspicion, in his voice which I did not like. I feared, his suspicions once aroused, that he would call for help : then good-bye to all hope of a peaceful elopement. There was nothing for it now but to seize the bull by the horns—but how ? The woman answered the unspoken question for me, and answered it in my own way. Drawing my face down to hers, she put her mouth to my ear and breathed, ' Kha,' at the same time doubling up my fist, which to her, no doubt, seemed big enough and strong enough to fell an elephant.

I was not slow to act upon the suggestion.

Placing the bundle on the floor, I stole from her side, and almost before he was aware of it I confronted him. When he saw me, a coolie in the women's quarters, his voice took a mighty horrid tone, and he actually raised his hand as though to strike. Now, it has always been a guiding principle of mine to get in, if possible, the first blow, and acting on this principle I let out : his nose came in contact with my knuckles, and over he went. But I had only injured, not stunned him, and as he rolled on the verandah he set up a most horrible howling. Knowing what this meant, and that in a minute or two we should have the whole place about our ears, I stepped back into the room and called, 'Pakna, Pakna!' She was instantly by my side, her hand in mine, and as we passed by the howling Kha she stopped for a second or two to administer sundry savage kicks and hiss out something decidedly unpleasant. I could not help smiling, serious as the position was.

The guide was already half through the shrubbery and brandishing his ugly knife in a way I did not like, especially as I knew he had a personal grudge against Kha. So I flung Pakna's bundle at him and told him to run and open the gate.

'Yes, mas'r,' he cried, but before obeying me he spat disdainfully towards the twisting figure, which continued to make a most infernal din. I had a great inclination to send him to sleep, and the rather trying position I was in might have justified the act; but I merely knelt on his stomach and gagged him with his own silk sash. Even that was too late. His howling had already roused the place. Voices, hurried, excited voices, called to each other from different parts of the building, while here and there lights began to flash. There was not a moment to lose, so I seized Pakna by the hand and hurried with all speed towards the gate. There stood my guide in readiness. As we approached, he opened the gate and we passed out, he following with a triumphant laugh.

By this time the shouts within the grounds had reached an alarming pitch, but fortunately we were on the right side of the wall. I gave the word forward, my guide and I with Pakna between us leading the way, my other two men, who joined us immediately we emerged from the garden, bringing up the rear. Pakna, being but a young woman, was as light of foot as either of us, so that we fairly bounded along the dark streets, never stopping to look round till we had reached the landing-stage.

Luckily the boat was in readiness. I stepped aboard and helped the woman after me, when she sank upon the seat shivering and crying and scarcely able to breathe ; at which I did not wonder, for I was fairly winded myself. Then the guide stepped aboard, followed by the rear-guard : I gave the order to push off, and we shot into the middle of the stream. And apparently none too soon, for, ere we had half cleared the little creek, a white-robed figure bounded on to the landing-stage we had just quitted and began wildly to shout at us. Soon this figure was joined by three or four others, and then a turn in the stream hid them from view.

I breathed more freely when we had cleared the creek and were fairly on the river, right down the middle of which I steered. The four rowers laid to with a good will, and for a time the banks seemed to skim by us ; but ours was a heavy, clumsy craft, a regular rough-

water boat, and required an amount of pro-
pulsion which meant the quick exhaustion of
muscular energy.   Still I kept them at full
pressure for a couple of miles, when of their
own accord they took an easy.   I kept a good
look-out ahead and astern, but fortunately no
pursuer hove in view.

Down past the shipping we flew, past the
buoys from which the old *Amoy* had cast loose
that very afternoon, and the free river stretched
before us.   I now regained my usual com-
posure, and, having partaken of a good pull
at the whisky-flask, I felt in such an excellent
humour that I could have bellowed a chanty
for very joy.

Happily the whisky had not absorbed all my
practical common-sense.   I was not yet out of
the wood: I could not feel the thousand dollars
nestling sweetly in my breast-pocket.   But, by
the Lord, I meant to.   I had no doubt now that
all pursuit was at an end.   The great adventure
had been accomplished in the most satisfactory
manner, and, feeling quite safe, I lit my pipe.
Then I called an easy to the men.   We had
plenty of time.   It would be two or three hours
yet before daybreak.

The woman all this time lay coiled up where she had at first fallen, and now that I had time to pay her a little attention I offered her a biscuit and some water, and told her in the best way I could that she had nothing more to fear. She looked up quite pitifully at me and shook her head. I laughingly shook mine in return, and motioned for her to eat; but, though she drank the water greedily, she only nibbled the biscuit. I told my guide to speak to her in the native tongue and reassure her; but he replied that she would not be reassured, as she still feared the vengeance of Kha. Knowing something of the perverseness of the sex, and how they will be just that which they are bent upon being, I left her to her own reflections and smoked away in silence.

In the meantime we had been floating quietly down the stream, the men resting on their oars. The moon was now out, and lit up the water ahead and astern to quite a considerable distance, so that, turning round for a last view before ordering the men on again, I caught the shadow of a moving object far astern. A moment or two of anxious scrutiny convinced me that the object was a boat, and that it was undoubtedly coming down-stream.   I gave the order coolly enough for the men to pull, but their quick eyes had discovered the object almost as soon as mine, and they needed no great urging.

For a while our boat fairly flew, but, travel as we would, we could not shake off the shadow astern ; and, as my men soon tired, the shadow began to gain on us in an alarming manner. Quickly seeing the futility of trying to show a clean pair of heels, and knowing how the effort would exhaust my men for the final tussle, I loosened my revolver, letting them see the action.   Then I ordered them to go easy. Profiting by my example, they also felt with one hand for their pistols, while with the other they made a pretence of rowing.   The woman, luckily, was as yet unconscious of the proximity of the pursuers, for she sat quite still, her head on her breast, her legs doubled up under her.

Soon the object was near enough for me to see that it was a big sampan with four oars going forward, while two men tugged desperately at the long steering-scull astern.   Our heavy boat had not a ghost of a chance with such a light, shallow thing propelled by half a dozen trained rowers.

As it came up astern of us hand over hand I hailed it, fearing it was their intention to run us down.

'Hullo, there!' I shouted. 'Look where you're coming!'

I was answered in the native tongue, my guide translating:

'What boat is that?'

'The gig of the steamship *Amoy*. What are you?'

For a moment there was no reply. Then the voice said, 'The *Amoy* left for Hong-Kong at half-past five this afternoon.'

'I know. We missed her. She is to wait for us at Koh-si-Chang. Go on, men.'

Away we went once more, but apparently without satisfying the people in the sampan, who immediately started in pursuit. The woman, clasping my knees, looked up imploringly into my face. She had heard what passed, and guessed its meaning; but I assured her that I would never give her up, and, though she did not comprehend a word of English, I am sure she understood me. She kissed my hand passionately and sank sobbing at my feet. I patted her head kindly, and covered her with my greatcoat.

But meanwhile the sampan had come close up astern, and the fellow in the bows hooked us with his boat-hook. With an angry exclamation I immediately sprang up and seized it, and, as I did so, a triumphant shout rose from the pursuers. This disconcerted me for the moment, though its meaning came to me like a flash. I had forgotten that I was still in native dress.

Then the sampan came alongside. They told us they knew who we were, and suggested that we might guess who they were: that they would not molest us if we gave up the woman, but in any case they meant to have her. I answered that I was sorry to disoblige them, but the woman had come into my hands, and I meant to keep her. I also warned them to sheer off lest harm befell them ; for, though I was a man of peace, I could not submit to the indignity of being dictated to by a bunch of niggers. They, however, took no heed of my warning. Therefore, still guided by my principle of having first shot, I fired at the sampan

M

just on the water-line, and think I must have put a couple of bullets through it. At all events there was a fearful spluttering and shouting, which excitement proving favourable to us, we sheered off and soon put a dozen boat's-lengths between us. But once their surprise was over, anger gave them courage, and with wild shouts they came dashing after us. I slipped a couple more cartridges into the empty chambers of my revolver, and then faced them.

On they came with awful yelling and shouting, apparently thinking to intimidate us by their ferocious cries. As they came within four or five boat's-lengths of us, my fear for our safety got the better of my discretion, and I emptied my revolver at them. This was answered by a heavy fire in return, though fortunately too high. I heard the bullets hiss through the air above me.

Then began a running fight, all my energies being concentrated upon hitting the boat in a serious place. Indeed, the better to take aim at her I exposed myself to some pretty shooting. But then I was not used to war, and, like a fool, thought nothing of cover. Indeed, one bullet tore the flesh from my shoulder : another laid low my guide, who dropped forward on his knees and held his hands to his side.   But the rowers swung on apparently uninjured, and I admired the coolness of the brave fellows.

But our pursuers, finding they got none the best of the exchanges at long range, now began rapidly to overhaul us, and, guessing their intention, I seized a spare oar and awaited the onslaught.   My men, watching my movements, loosened their sheath-knives.   I saw their eyes gleam.   Even the guide, wounded as he was, seized his boat-hook and stood on guard.

In a moment they were on us.   The two boats ground against each other ominously. Then a fearful confusion followed.   There was an indiscriminate smashing of oars, a flashing of knives, a babel of voices.   The screeching was something horrid.   I laid about me with my great oar, and made more than one worthy coolie grunt.   The man next to me used his as a spear, and poked the sharp, solid handle at his adversaries.   The others used their knives or oars as best they could, and for about three minutes a furious fight ensued.

Then suddenly a great cry of alarm came

from the sampan. Their boat was surely sinking. In their excitement they had evidently not noticed it, but now there could no longer be any doubt. The sampan was going down by the head. They therefore sheered off immediately, and the battle ceased. Whether the sampan sank or not I cannot say, for no sooner were they well clear of us than we pushed forward on our journey.

My guide was wounded seriously, while all the other men had more or less received hard knocks ; but we did what we had to do, and in the early haze of the following morning the old *Amoy* picked us up.

CHIEF OFFICER GROVER

FOR over two months we had swung idly at anchor in the harbour of Hong-Kong. Business in the shipping world had been exceedingly slack, and when a tramp came in to discharge she was never sure when she would go out again. Our last voyage had been from Nagasaki with coal. Accordingly, after getting rid of that objectionable stuff, we had plenty of time to clean up. For the rest, our hull made a good anchorage for the barnacles.

But one day the captain came aboard and sent for the chief officer, and then the news leaked out that we were presently to make a move. We had been chartered to run down to Saigon, load up with rice, and return to Hong-Kong—a voyage, at the longest, of three weeks' duration. I for one should have preferred Bombay or Sydney, but the fiat had gone forth, and Saigon it was to be.

The person who had chartered us was one Ah Yeh, a well-known merchant on the island, and, so some said, much better known than respected. But be that as it may, Ah Yeh was a man of considerable wealth and influence, and as such held a responsible position in the commercial world. A man who can meet present liabilities need not fear his antecedents; and if Ah Yeh had any black marks against his name, no one cared to remind him of them. Yet some curious tales were set afloat concerning him. It was said that he had originally been a sampan coolie, and that by dint of super-excellence in cunning he had risen to be one of the foremost native merchants of South China. But there is usually a stiff price paid for greatness, and Ah Yeh's case was no exception to the rule. Success brought its attendant evils, which Ah Yeh declared were killing him; and yet he throve and waxed fat.

On the two or three occasions I had the honour of visiting him at his office, I found him particularly charming. He came out into the shop when he knew I was there, asked me into his inner sanctum, cracked a pint of champagne, and filled my case with cigars.

Speaking in excellent English, and with a peculiarly soft and winning accent, he began to question me about the ship, displaying a great interest in all that pertained to the life of a sailor. I can see him now as he put his questions, his smooth, yellow, not unhandsome face all aglow with intelligence, and a motive I could not then fathom; his little black eyes dancing into mine, the long nail on the little finger of his left hand with which he lovingly scratched the tip of his nose. I remember, though thinking little of it then, the stress he laid on the dangers of a voyage to Saigon, particularly when near the Paracels. He had heard of those rocks, of the many vessels that had rushed upon them to their doom; and in his innocent, earnest fashion he wanted to know if I was very much afraid of them. I laughed at the idea, and Ah Yeh laughed too, but there was not much spontaneity or mirth about it. And then, with the same appearance of extreme innocence, he wondered if ships were sometimes wrecked on purpose, and what remuneration a responsible officer expected for the work. I did not answer, and Ah Yeh, smiling more insinuatingly than ever, said he should be pleased to hear my views on the subject. Appealed to thus, I spoke somewhat hotly on the matter, and in a very few moments I knew I had a most inattentive listener. Then Ah Yeh rose rather brusquely and told me he would be pleased to see me the next time I was passing that way. One is naturally wiser after the event, though it seems absurd that I should have thought so little about my cross-examination. In the face of what happened, it seems incredible that my perception should have failed so lamentably.

The day before we sailed, Ah Yeh sent aboard a supercargo and half a dozen clerks, and a villainous-looking batch they were, the supercargo in particular with his flat cheeks, flat forehead, and flat eyes being a most forbidding blackguard. But ugliness being the common heritage of the Mongol, one soon begins to pass it by without comment. Ah Yeh's yellow batch was, after all, no serious libel on the country.

Well, early the following morning, away we went, and during the voyage down nothing of an eventful nature befell us. The weather was comfortably cool, the sea smooth, and, though we were no great shakes at speed, we made fairly good progress, though the barnacles we had accumulated in Hong-Kong impeded us somewhat.

Very little was seen of the supercargo or his assistants. Occasionally they appeared on deck, but the greater part of the time they spent below gambling and smoking. There was, however, one exception. The supercargo, Wong, was a man of an inquiring turn of mind, and seemed to take considerable interest in affairs aboard. At first he tried to hobnob with me, but when he found that I wouldn't have any truck with him, he sought out the mate, and I watched with some degree of disgust the intimacy between them ripen. To be sure, everything was done secretly, but two or three times I had surprised them drinking together in the mate's cabin, and, by the guilty way my superior officer started, I knew that he was ashamed of himself. Nor was it whisky or rum that they drank, nor any such common sailor's tipple, but champagne—good whizzing, fizzing champagne. Of course I knew how the stuff got there—indeed, the triumphant gleam of Wong's flat eyes assured me ; but it was not my place to remonstrate with my chief. I might deplore the circumstance, but could do nothing more.

Our mate was rather a common type of sailor-man, the kind of fellow you would expect to hear had begun life forward, but by dint of perseverance had succeeded in getting his ticket. How he ever got it was always a wonder to me, for he was a singularly faulty navigator and not a particularly clever seaman. His appearance was not prepossessing. Indeed, it rather foolishly made you take a dislike to the man at first sight. There is, however, nothing romantic about a short, thickset figure, and without doubt Mr. Grover's figure was both short and thickset; and, though he carried his big head well forward, as though his neck were too weak to bear it, I can vouch for the exceeding stoutness of that neck. A black, untrimmed beard spread itself over his face right up to his eyes, which eyes, and a short, red protuberance which he called his nose, were his only visible features. Not an attractive man, perhaps, and yet such was a very fair outline of Mr. Daniel Grover, chief officer of the s.s. *Malacca*.

He had not been with us for more than five

months; and though I don't think he ever gave the old man any great cause for satisfaction, he never, as far as I'm aware, gave him any serious cause for uneasiness. We had picked Mr. Grover up in Singapore, and, though a good man may occasionally be found there, it is not the best of ports to hail from. Good, reliable men, as a rule, are not found stranded in the East; men of a certain class are to be found in any number. Grover's discharge must have been all right or the old man would never have taken him; though I have known skippers so hard pressed at times that they were glad enough to take anything they could get. At any rate, Grover joined us at Singapore, and I was not sufficiently in the captain's confidence to know the why or the wherefore. I only know that we wanted a chief mate, and that Mr. Daniel Grover came aboard. Though his appearance was against him, he and I got on very well together — for a few weeks. He seemed a bluff, hearty, good-natured sort of sailor-man with no pretension to class; and, after all, class is not of the utmost importance to those who go down to the sea in tramps. He appeared to be a decent enough fellow, and that was sufficient. Before we left the Japan ports, I knew Mr. Daniel Grover for quite a different sort of person.

But in the meantime I have left the ship rapidly approaching Saigon, which port we duly reached, and, when we had loaded, as duly cleared again. True, Grover, during the operation of loading, did not forget to cultivate his intimacy with the supercargo Wong; but nothing of any moment happened till we were clear of the river. Then, when everything was going well above, the captain having set the course and gone below, leaving the third in charge of the bridge, I went to look the chief up, and found him squatting on his bunk, his legs dangling over the side, a pipe in his mouth, and a tumbler of champagne in his hand. The supercargo Wong was squatting on the settee opposite, his legs curled up under him, a tumbler in one hand, a bottle of champagne in the other, and a cheroot stuck between his thick lips, the thin end protruding.

'Come in, Emson,' cried the mate cheerily, as soon as he caught sight of me; 'come in, man, and have a glass of grog. You look as miserable as a flayed bloater, damn me if you don't! Here, Wong, you soor, tip up the rum!'

'None, thanks ; not just now,' I said, seeing that my respected chief was already three sheets in the wind, and having no wish to fraternise with the curious Wong.

'Rot!' shouted the mate. 'Tip it up, Wong, you soor!'

'Welly good,' said Mr. Wong insinuatingly, making the bubbles dance in the glass as he held it out to me. 'This lum allee same belong first chop. Same as Cap'n dlink when he go see top-side girlee,' and out of his little flat eyes he gave me an intensely knowing look. The mate roared hilariously at the joke, and with his heels beat an excited tatoo on the locker.

'This Wong's a soor,' he said admiringly, 'but he does carry the right stuff and no mistake. Now, Emson, drink up. Here's a prosperous voyage to the good ship *Malacca*, and may she never go to the bottom till her insurance will make it worth her while!'

'I dlink,' said Mr. Wong, 'to the good ship *Malacca*.' And as he emptied his tumbler, he looked at the mate in a way that made me feel quite sick.

'Now, Emson,' cried that worthy, evidently determined that I should join the carousal, 'you can't with decency refuse to drink such a toast.'

'I never drink champagne,' I said.

'Neither do I,' he grinned, 'especially when I can't get it. But what, may I ask, is your especial tipple, Mr. Particular?'

'It all depends on the occasion,' I replied.

'Oh, I see,' he sneered, 'we ain't good enough for you. Wong's a blasted Chink, and I'm a——'

'Blasted fool!'

He sprang off his bunk, his eyes blazing with anger, and, shaking a hairy fist in my face, roared, 'Look here, Mr.—Particular, for two pins I'd flatten you! Son of a sea-cook!' he growled. 'Bah! they breed better men than you on a Thames penny-packet.'

'And cast them adrift at Singapore,' I said.

His flushed eyes grew very searching as he looked into my face.

'What do you mean?' he muttered.

'Just what you like,' I answered; 'and when we get to Hong-Kong I'll trouble you to step across to the Kowloon side and repeat in my

face what you have just now said.' With that
I turned and quitted the cabin, a string of
infamous oaths following me along the alley-
way.

Nothing of any consequence happened for
the next two days. He had always an ugly
look for me, and he gave his orders in much
the way that a man would speak to a dog ; but
his tone of voice was a thing I could not very
well resent ; moreover, he was my superior
officer, and discipline forbade any questioning
on my part. As for the curious Wong, he kept
himself out of the way as much as possible,
though I knew that he and the mate were still
as thick as thieves.

I being the second officer always took the
middle watch, and on the third morning out, a
minute or two after eight bells had struck, the
mate duly made his appearance to relieve me.
I was standing in the starboard corner of the
bridge at the time, keeping a good look-out,
and thinking of the proximity of the Paracels,
when he stepped over to me. As soon as he
spoke I knew he had been drinking heavily.
His voice vibrated shockingly as he asked me
if I had seen anything.

'No,' I answered, as civilly as I could, 'but we can't be very far off. The captain cautions a good look-out, and says he is to be called immediately anything is seen.'

I think he resented my tone of imparting information, for he muttered something uncomplimentary under his breath and then lurched across to the binnacle. I immediately descended the bridge.

But, instead of going straight to my cabin, I stood for a minute or two looking hard out across the starboard bow, and thinking in a persistent irritating sort of way of the dangerous shoals lying out yonder; for, try as I would, I could not disconnect them and the man on the bridge. Of course I knew my misgivings were the very height of absurdity, but as I peered out into the darkness I entertained some most distressing thoughts.

Presently I heard the mate speak to the man at the wheel, his coarse voice easily reaching where I stood:

'What's she steering, quartermaster?'

I could not catch the reply, though I knew quite well what it would be. There was a moment's pause. Then the mate spoke again:

'Are you quite sure?'

'Quite, sir. That's as Johnson gave it to me.' Johnson was the quartermaster whom this man had relieved.

I heard the mate mutter something, and then I knew by the direction his voice took that he had gone into the chart-room.

For a while nothing was heard but the grind, grind of the screw, the splash of the waves as they fell back from the ship's bows. Then presently the mate emerged from the chart-room, and, after taking half a dozen excited turns up and down the bridge, he stopped alongside the binnacle, and I distinctly heard him say, 'Just run down for my pipe, quartermaster. You'll find it on the shelf above my bunk.'

'Yes, sir,' answered the man. There was a shuffling of feet, and I knew that the mate had taken the wheel.

Beneath the bridge there was a small wheel-house, with an auxiliary steering-wheel which was only to be used if anything happened to the gear above. This house, though now converted into a lamp-room by the quartermasters, was, according to custom, kept ready for use

N

in case of necessity. Everything was ready and in its proper order—even to the binnacle lamp being lit.

Into this house, then, I slipped as soon as I heard the quartermaster clatter down the ladder, and, as if impelled by some intuition, I sprang towards the binnacle and gazed eagerly in at the compass. What my thoughts were may, perhaps, be guessed ; but I was conscious of the wave of relief that passed through me when I saw that we were still on our course. I had evidently misjudged Mr. Chief Officer Grover : had done that honest man a most grievous injury. Well, the best of us may err at times, and, if I had judged Mr. Grover harshly, he had only himself to thank for——

I started, leaving the thought unfinished, my eyes riveted to the face of the compass. One — two — three — four points it swung to the eastward, and then it steadied. I watched it breathlessly to see if it would swing back again. But no. The mate, on his own initiative, had actually altered the course of the vessel four points, and she was now steadied at that! I could scarcely believe my eyes, credit my senses. I looked closer ;

I pinched myself to see if I were dreaming: but no, there was no longer any doubt. The ship's course was altered. Why? For what? I trembled as I thought of the answer such a question suggested. Chief Officer Grover had taken upon himself a dreadful responsibility. He had neither orders nor authority for altering the course of the ship. Indeed, such an alteration was fraught with incalculable danger. The last thing the captain said to me that night before he turned in was, 'Tell Mr. Grover to keep her on this course, and don't forget to let me know if you see anything.' Indeed, with the Paracels lying so close to the eastward of us, the mate had been guilty of a most reprehensible act, and I knew there would be a pretty set-out when the old man heard of it in the morning.

However, it was no affair of mine, and, as I was not anxious to cultivate the reputation of a sneak, I, after waiting till the quartermaster returned, went below. But sleep I could not. Whenever I closed my eyes I thought I saw the ship running over the land at express speed, steered by a gibbering demon who eventually took unto himself the shape of Mr.

Chief Officer Grover. Once I thought we were sailing upside down, as ships do in a mirage, and that upon the keel, with a glass in his hand and a pipe in his mouth, sat our worthy chief grinning diabolically at me. This was more than mere human flesh could bear. It was bad enough to dream of the ship cutting such extraordinary capers, but it was intolerable to be haunted by the presence of the mate. So, by way of relaxation, I got up and had a squint through the port.

The day was still a long way off, but it was surely breaking somewhere in the east, and through the early morning mists I felt almost sure that I could hear the low booming of far-off breakers. I listened, listened intently. But what with the grinding of the screw, the thump, thump of the engines, and the noise made by the water as it rushed hissing by, I was sorely confused. Moreover, strung as I was to such a pitch of excitement, I was readily persuaded to doubt my own hearing. And yet, sleep being entirely out of the question, I hurriedly filled a pipe, as a pretence for showing up, and then went on deck in my pyjamas.

Advancing to the starboard side, I leant on

the rail and tried to pierce the misty distance; but nothing coming of it, I turned my eyes towards the bridge. A moment or two of intense scrutiny, and then I became conscious of the fact that several forms were flitting about on the port side a little abaft of that structure. I watched anxiously, scarcely knowing why, and then I thought I heard the mate's voice. This was immediately followed by the creaking of tackle. What could this mean? Scarcely giving myself time to think, I hurried round to the other side, and surprised the curious Wong and his half-dozen clerks straining every muscle to swing out the port lifeboat. The mate was giving his orders in hoarse whispers from his stand on the bridge.

Almost before they were aware of what had happened, I was in their midst.

'Hallo, what's this?' I exclaimed. 'Who gave you the orders to launch that boat?'

There was a moment or two of silence, and then the ingenuous Wong stepped forward.

'Orders,' he lisped, in his innocent, baby fashion, 'Wong no sabbee orders.'

'Who's that?' cried the mate, coming to the bridge ladder and peering down at us.

'I—Emson.'

'Well, what do you want?' he growled.

'Do you know these fellows are swinging out one of the lifeboats?'

'What business is that of yours?'

'I should like to know who gave them the order.'

'That's my affair,' he bawled. 'It's your watch below. What do you want sneaking about the decks?'

'It's time to be about when you are getting ready the boats,' I replied. 'When do you expect her to strike?'

'Damn you!' he muttered, 'you will insist on crossing me! Look out—you'll cross me once too often. Now go below and mind your own —— business.'

'I think I had better first tell the captain that you have altered the ship's course four points to the eastward. He might be interested in the movement.'

I could not see the mate's face, but I imagined it by the silence that followed. Then he shambled down the ladder and came to me.

'What do you mean by that?' he asked under his breath.

'You know well enough.'

Continuing to advance, he said, 'You're too clever for me, Mr. Emson. I think we shall have to part company.'

'Keep back!' I cried, guessing the man's horrible design, and seizing one of the long, heavy rowlocks of the boat; 'if you lay a hand on me I'll brain you.'

'Then own that you're a liar—that you don't know what you're talking about.'

'I know perfectly well what I'm talking about.'

'Then there's only one way with sneaks. Wong, close up.'

I saw the hideous wretches form a semi-circle round me—my back was to the rail—and in another moment I knew I should see the glimmer of their knives. Then, just as I was on the point of charging, I heard the old man's voice ring out distinct and clear.

'Hullo! what the blazes is the matter here?'

The Chinamen instantly fell back; the mate hung his head and muttered incoherently. The captain was only one podgy little man, but he had the moral influence of twenty.

'Mr. Grover has ordered out the lifeboat, sir.'

'Eh?' said the old man, in a tone which threw discredit on his hearing.

I repeated the information.

'Lifeboat—ordered out,' mumbled he. Then, seeming to grasp the situation, he turned sharply to the chief officer. 'What does this mean, Mr. Grover?'

'It means that I ain't going to risk my damned skin for you nor twenty like you,' bawled the mate defiantly.

'Mr. Grover, sir,' said the captain, 'by God, sir, I never allow an officer of mine to speak to me like that.'

'Then what do you want to hug the damned land for?' yelled the mate, whose desperate position had endowed him with a desperate courage.

'Hug the land, sir?' repeated the bewildered captain.

'Yes, sir, hug the land, sir,' said the mate, imitating him.

'Go below to your room, sir,' roared the old man. 'You're drunk, sir, drunk.'

'As you must have been, I reckon, when you set this ship's course.'

The captain stood speechless, his stodgy

form quivering with anger. Then he began
to splutter, but he hadn't got further than
'You infernal scoundrel,' when he stopped
short and cocked up his stodgy little ears. A
moment only he listened, we all listened, and
then the ominous boom, boom of breakers was
heard on our starboard bow. The old man
sprang forward with a cry, and as he mounted
the ladder of the bridge he screamed out:

'Starboard, starboard—hard a-starboard!'

'Hard a-starboard it is, sir,' answered the
quartermaster, as he sent the wheel spinning
and jammed it down. The nose of the ship
slewed round to the west, and apparently not
a moment too soon. As the bank of mist on
our right suddenly lifted, I saw, not a hundred
yards from us, a cluster of low black rocks—
and we had been rushing straight upon them!

The captain then called for me to join him
on the bridge, the mate, nothing daunted,
following at my heels.

'Come here, Emson,' said the old man, 'I
want to speak to you. As for you, Mr. Grover,
you will please retire to the chart-room till
you're wanted.'

'What for?' growled the mate.

'Damn you, because I tell you!'

The mate slouched off with a very poor grace, and the captain, beckoning me aside, heard all I had to tell.

Yes, the whole story came out at the trial: how, for the sake of the insurance, Grover had entered into an arrangement with Wong to wreck the ship, for which crime he was to receive two thousand dollars. Ah Yeh, however, who was rightly called the clever one, stoutly denied any knowledge of the affair, and he had so guarded himself that no guilt could be laid to his charge.

Mr. Chief Officer Grover will not be able to go to sea again for seven years.

SAYŌNARA

WHEN Vershiel first saw Hina-San she was romping in the garden of one of the big tea-houses of Kobe, playing, with a child of six or seven, a sort of battledore and shuttlecock. The peal upon peal of laughter which came from behind the big wistaria tree first attracted the man's attention. Wondering what could be the cause of so much merriment, he stole out into the grounds, and, behold, there was Hina-San in her white tabi, her face flushed, her eyes dancing with happiness. A pretty, plump, innocent-looking little thing, entering into the childish game with all the earnestness and energy of a child. For a few moments the man watched unobserved, watched with a cold, critical eye, letting no point of the view escape him. Then, with a smile on his face and a clapping of hands, he advanced into view.

The applause was the tribute paid to Hina-

San's skill and agility, and she smiled pleasantly, thinking it came from one of her companions; but when she saw the stranger advance, the flush on her face grew deeper, and she hung her head like a child caught doing a naughty thing.

Vershiel, still continuing to advance, smiled encouragingly at her, and nodded for her to continue her game; but she only hung her head and began to giggle.

'Then if you won't play,' he said, 'will you bring me some tea out here in the garden?'

She nodded, smiling: shuffled her feet into her straw sandals, and toddled off.

The man walked to a seat beneath the big wistaria, and, resting his face in his hands, watched the white clouds fluttering over the hill-tops. But did he see those clouds, note the sloping outline of the hills? or did he see anything but a palpitating bit of humanity in a cream kimono?

As she stood before him, the little tea-tray in her hands, the warm flush filling her face with sweetness, he found himself half wondering if the scene were real. But not alone was it real—it was a charming reality. He spoke, and she answered with a smile. He thought he had never seen such pretty teeth. The mouth too, full and red, met with his entire approval. Indeed, the more he looked the more wonderful he thought it that a native woman should be so attractive, and he found himself thinking strange things about this pretty, odd creature. A *mousmee*, a tea-girl—an ignorant little thing who played baby games with all the ardour of a baby. And yet a woman.

Vershiel had not been long in Japan, nor was it expected that he would make a long stay. Business alone had brought him there, and, that business accomplished, he would depart. But, for all he knew to the contrary, he might be detained in Kobe for another six months, and he had been warned to beware of promiscuous loves.

He was very careful with Hina-San at first, knowing how easily terrified these little creatures are; but in her eyes he was a godlike personage, in whose presence she was scarcely fit to breathe, and, though he remained a god to the last, he was a god to whom she had grown accustomed.

Then came the interview with her parents and considerable haggling over the sum they were willing to take for a loan of their daughter for, say, six months. Hina-San herself felt flattered and honoured : flattered that the white stranger should condescend to look upon one so insignificant and unworthy, honoured that he should esteem her so greatly as to get her to come and keep house for him. The white stranger thought—but perhaps we had better not inquire into his thoughts. He did what every fellow who could afford it did, and, egad! he was deuced good to her.

Vershiel's nature was a purely business one, coldly calculating and extremely punctilious. A business arrangement was simply a business arrangement. If he promised to pay so many yen per month for an article, he considered that article his while he fulfilled the contract. There was no other obligation. As for sentiment—well, everybody knew that sentiment and the native women were as widely separated as the poles. True, he had no fault to find with Hina-San. The Japanese woman seems born for housekeeping, and Vershiel's housekeeper, as a housekeeper, was perfection. When the

bills for the first month came in, he was so
astounded at her success that he straightway
declared a dividend in favour of her and her
parents. But here his interest in her ceased.
As a companion she was a mere cipher—an
interesting one, it is true, but a cipher nevertheless. He did not seem to think it possible
that she might grow foolishly attached to him.
He recognised her obligations ; but for anything else he hadn't a second thought.

And yet her poor, ignorant little breast was
full of love for him. If he touched her, the
blood bounded through her veins with sickening
rushes ; if he carelessly flung an arm about her
shoulders, every pulse in her body went throb,
throb, till it seemed as though it would snap
with the tension. Sometimes he kissed her,
but not often. He admitted that he never
cared for those curious-lidded dark brown eyes.
Yet had he looked, looked with the thinking
eye, he would have seen devotion inexpressible,
love transcending all thought of earth. He
saw only the peculiar lids, the ugly slits through
which the eyes shone. And she, being but an
ignorant, honest girl, was only half-conscious
of the great devotion that had come to her.

She knew that for her there was but one god, and that Vershiel was his name. But as the devout would approach God with fear and trembling, so she approached her master; and if he read not her heart, saw not the love in those eyes, how could she tell him?

And so the weeks and the months flew by, Hina-San leading an enchanted life; for he had grown kinder to her of late—perchance for more reasons than one: but whatever his reasons were, his kindness was received as a token of the master's pleasure in his hand-maiden, and she went blithely to and fro. Then the time came when he had to break the news of his intending departure. The six months of their contract had elapsed: he was going away to Yokohama, and she must go back to her people.

She listened to him like one who hears but does not comprehend. Then her face grew suddenly white, and with a little heartbroken sob she turned away. She could not have told him what she felt, even if she could have formed the words—it would have been taking too great a liberty with her honourable lord. She could only steal away and bury her face

in her hands: wonder at the strange lump in
her throat, the sudden chill that enwrapped
her heart: marvel at the awful coldness and
emptiness of the world. An hour ago the sun
was shining, the world was full of light and
loveliness: now the great lamp had gone out,
and the winter storms were howling round the
desolate dwelling.

Vershiel thought he could sever the con-
nection as easily as he had made it. He gave
her lots of money, he heaped presents upon her
and her people; he did all that a generous
business man could do, and marvelled much at
her apathy. He did not seem to take into
account the woman's great love, her unselfish
devotion, or the fact that ere long she would
be a mother. Not knowing the love, he could
not feel the regret: the unselfish devotion
would have made him smile. How was he
to know that the girl valued the money so
little that she never kept a yen of it, but
handed it over intact to her parents? As for
the motherhood—that was a trifling inconvenience which she and her people would have to
see to. Moreover, he doubted the story, or
doubted what they would have him believe.

How could he credit her honesty?   His friends laughed heartily at the mere suggestion.   It was always the last card, they said.   Every-body had had a similar experience; but a few yen always smoothed the difficulty.

And so, despite her tears, entreaties, and the hopeless pathos of her brown eyes, he said *sayōnara* (farewell), and went away, and by emptying his purse in her lap thought he had discharged all obligations.   To be sure, there was the half-promise to come back, wrung from him in a moment of weakness to alleviate her distress; but it was a promise he had no real intention of fulfilling, and as such it sat lightly on his conscience.   It mattered nothing that the poor, ignorant girl hugged it madly to her soul, that joy unspeakable darted to her pathetic eyes as she pictured the joyous home-coming: it mattered nothing, this breaking of a native woman's heart.

She went back to her people, rich, laden with presents, and was petted and made much of while the riches lasted; but the pettings of home, the love of interested parents, were probably accepted at their proper value.   It all helped to make the long, dreary days pass till he returned, and to make those days pass was now her only object in life. But day ran to week, and week to month, and yet he came not. Still she bore up bravely, believing in that promise, though her face grew paler and thinner, and the pathos in her eyes more pitiful. 'He will come,' she whispered consolingly to herself; 'he will come in time to welcome the little one—our little one. He is great, he is good, and he will not forget his Hina-San, his little Hina-San. Oh, my beloved, come, come!' And the little plump brown hands went out entreatingly, and the brown pathetic eyes shone sadly through the blinding tears.

And so day succeeded day, and at last the little one came; and when her people saw that it was a white man's child they hated it with a mad, unreasoning hatred, bitterly censuring their daughter for her stupidity. But to her who had loved the father, the wee thing came in time to save her brain from bursting, her heart from breaking. Every drop of white blood that ran in its veins was sacred to her— a sacred link connecting her with the never-to-be-forgotten past.

But when her money was spent, and one by

one her trinkets had gone, and she was once more as poor as in the days when Vershiel first saw her, then began the bitter tauntings of her people. And they said, 'Cast out the brat of this white man, this thief who leaves you both to perish. Why shouldst thou carry about this living shame, so that all who see may mock at thee and us? A curse on him and all his race! Nothing but misery have the white men brought to our land.' And they grew wroth with her because she paid no heed to them. But to her the child was dearer, far dearer than life. For every precious drop of white blood that coursed through its tiny veins she would have died a dozen deaths. There was something more than pathos in the brown eyes now.

But they were cruel days of waiting, and poor Hina-San grew pale and weary, and the child languished in consequence. Then was it her people bade her go forth, she and her shame ; and never again did they see her, or hear the voice of the white shame cry—except in their dreams.

With her baby on her back she tramped to the tea-house where she had first met Vershiel, and, in consequence of good service, she was reinstalled in her old position. But it was no longer the Hina-San of old who came back, not the Hina-San who had romped childishly with the child, not the rosy-faced girl who had brought the tea to the white stranger beneath the big wistaria. A dozen times she went over the scene. There were the seat and the table just as they had been a year ago, there was the big tree a mass of blossom. She shut her eyes and tried to fancy he was sitting there, just as he had sat that day. She brought her white shame and sat him in the seat of his father, and even as she looked her vision grew blurred, and the one word, 'Yokohama,' the word that had haunted her for months past, started to her lips. Yes, she would go to Yokohama; she had long thought of it: now her mind was made up. It seemed a terrible journey, a fearful undertaking; but she would go, and, when he heard her story, saw him whom her people called the white shame, he would surely take her back to him as in the old days.

So, when she had saved enough money to pay her passage to Yokohama, she went down to one of the big steamers, and they stowed her away somewhere between-decks, she and her white shame; and she knew little more till they came to tell her that the ship had arrived at Yokohama.

Yokohama! She awoke from her long dream, allowed them to lead her up the companion, and down into a small boat. Then they rowed her across the water to the hatoba, and as she walked up the steps, her white shame slung on her back, they told her that she was in Yokohama.

Yokohama! She gazed round bewildered. Yokohama at last! The place he had come to, the place where he lived! Now all her troubles were over : she had come to Yokohama —to him!

For hours she wandered about repeating the name 'Vershiel—Mr. Vershiel,' but all to whom she spoke stared at her with curious insolence, or laughed outright in her face. But one, more kind than the others, who saw the agony in her eyes, told her to go to the European quarter and inquire, and even took the trouble to show her the way. There she learnt that Mr. Vershiel, who belonged to one of the biggest houses in Japan, had long since sailed

for England. England! The thought almost
staggered her. England, that land beyond
the sea, beyond the sun—beyond the world, it
seemed. Her voice grew tremulous, her sad
eyes full of agony. When had he gone? Many
months ago in the s.s. *Hakodate*. *Hakodate*,
ha! She would remember that name. And
when would the *Hakodate* be back? They could
not say, but probably at the end of the year.

So away she went, sore at heart and yet
clinging to her last fond hope. She procured
lodgings, found employment, and then set
herself to keep her long vigil. The *Hakodate* would surely come back one day, and
that day she must be there to hear the good
news. So every evening, when her work was
done, she slung her white shame across her
shoulders and walked from the native quarter
to the English hatoba, and asked the sampan
men if the *Hakodate* had yet arrived; and
when they said no, she turned about and
toddled back murmuring, 'To-morrow, to-morrow—perhaps he will come to-morrow.'

But the to-morrows came and went, the
weeks ran into months, and yet the ship came
not. But one evening, a cold stormy night,

as she arrived pale and shivering at the hatoba, she saw a boat coming ashore from a big ship which evidently had just arrived ; and one of the sampan men called out to her—for they all knew her and her quest by this time—'That big ship yonder is the *Hakodate*.' She heard him and trembled, but it was with a joy that almost frightened her.

As the boat approached the landing-stage she watched it intently, and saw that there were several white men aboard it, but her eyes grew so dim with tears that she could not make out their faces. Eagerly, but vainly, she sought to clear her eyes ; nor till the men had come up the steps and were close upon her did she see that he was not there. Then she stepped forward to one, the one who had given her the information upon her first arrival in Yohohama, and cried out, 'Vershiel—Mr. Vershiel—have he no come ?'

The man started ; then, recognising her, said, 'No, my poor woman—Mr. Vershiel is in England.'

'But—he—will—come ?' The slow, broken English was full of hesitation—of hesitation and intense pain.

'Mr. Vershiel will never come to Japan again.'

'Not come—not come?'

But the man shook his head at the pathetic little figure and marched on.

Early the next morning some fishermen discovered the bodies of a woman and a child floating some three miles above the settlement. The child was clasped in the woman's arms. In the bosom of the woman's kimono they found the photograph of a somewhat sinister though decidedly good-looking European. Across the back of the card was written in native characters the one word, 'Sayōnara.'

Printed by T. and A. CONSTABLE, Printers to Her Majesty
at the Edinburgh University Press

John Lane

The Bodley Head

VIGO STREET, LONDON, W.

THE KEYNOTES SERIES.

Each volume with Designed Title-page and Cover
Crown 8vo.   3s. 6d. net.

Seventh Edition.

KEYNOTES.   By GEORGE EGERTON.   Crown 8vo, 3s. 6d.
net.

'This is a collection of eight of the prettiest short stories that have appeared for many a day.   They turn for the most part on feminine traits of
character ; in fact, the book is a little psychological study of woman under
various circumstances.   The characters are so admirably drawn, and the
scenes and landscapes are described with so much and so rare vividness,
that one cannot help being almost spell-bound by their perusal.'—*St. James's
Gazette.*

'A rich, passionate temperament vibrates through every line. . . . We
have met nothing so lovely in its tenderness since Mr. Kipling's "Without
Benefit of Clergy."'—*Daily Chronicle.*

'For any one who cares more for truth than for orthodox mummery, and
for the real flood of the human heart than for the tepid negus which stirs
the veins of respectability, this little book deserves a hearty welcome.'
—*Sketch.*

'These lovely sketches are informed by such throbbing feeling, such insight into complex woman, that we with all speed and warmth advise those
who are in search of splendid literature to procure "Keynotes" without
delay.'—*Literary World.*

'The work of a woman who has lived every hour of her life, be she young
or old. . . . She allows us, like the great artists of old, Shakespeare and
Goethe, to draw our own moral from the stories she tells, and it is with no
uncertain touch or faltering hand that she pulls aside the curtain of con-
ventional hypocrisy which hundreds of women hang between the world and
their own hearts. . . . The insight of the writer into the curious and com-
plicated nature of women is almost miraculous.'—*Lady's Pictorial.*

THE DANCING FAUN. By FLORENCE FARR. Crown 8vo, 3s. 6d. net.

'There is a lurid power in the very unreality of the story. One does not quite understand how Lady Geraldine worked herself up to shooting her lover, but when she has done it, the description of what passes through her mind is magnificent.'—*Athenæum.*

'As a work of art the book has the merit of brevity and smart writing; while the *dénoûement* is skilfully prepared, and comes as a surprise. If the book had been intended as a satire on the "new woman" sort of literature, it would have been most brilliant; but assuming it to be written in earnest, we can heartily praise the form of its construction without agreeing with the sentiments expressed.'—*St. James's Gazette.*

'Written by an obviously clever woman.'—*Black and White.*

'Miss Farr has talent. "The Dancing Faun" contains writing that is distinctively good. Doubtless it is only a prelude to something much stronger.'—*Academy.*

'The book is extremely clever and some of the situations very striking, while there are sketches of character which really live. The final *dénoûement* might at first sight be thought impossible, but the effect on those who take part in it is so free of exaggeration, that we can almost imagine that such people are in our midst.'—*Guardian.*

POOR FOLK. Translated from the Russian of FEDOR DOSTOIEVSKY. By LENA MILMAN. With an Introduction by GEORGE MOORE. Crown 8vo, 3s. 6d. net.

'A most impressive and characteristic specimen of Russian fiction. Those to whom Russia is a sealed book will be duly grateful to the translator (who has acquitted herself excellently), to Mr. Moore, and to the publisher for this presentment of Dostoievsky's remarkable novel.'—*Times.*

'The book is cleverly translated. "Poor Folk" gains in reality and pathos by the very means that in less skilful hands would be tedious and commonplace.'—*Spectator.*

'A charming story of the love of a Charles Lamb kind of old bachelor for a young work-girl. Full of quiet humour and still more full of the *lachrymæ rerum.*'—*Star.*

'Scenes of poignant realism, described with so admirable a blending of humour and pathos that they haunt the memory.'—*Daily News.*

'The book is one of great pathos and absorbing interest. Miss Milman has given us an admirable version of it which will commend itself to every one who cares for good literature.'—*Glasgow Herald.*

'These things seem small, but in the hands of Dostoievsky they make a work of genius. —*Black and White.*

A CHILD OF THE AGE. By FRANCIS ADAMS. Crown 8vo, 3s. 6d. net.

'The book is packed with vivid interests of all kinds, passages of noble reflection and beautiful, passionate writing. It is rarely that a novelist is able to suffuse his story with the first rosy purity of passion as Mr. Adams has done in this book, the tragic end of which is one of the most moving things to be found in recent fiction.'—*Realm.*

'In "A Child of the Age" there is prevalent power, there is frequent beauty, but its main charm lies in its revelation of a personality which, if not always winning, is certainly always fascinating and impressive.'—*Daily Chronicle.*

'English or foreign, there is no work among those now before me which is so original as that of the late Francis Adams. "A Child of the Age" is original, moving, often fascinating.'—*Academy.*

'It comes recognisably near to great excellence. There is a love episode in this book which is certainly fine. Clearly conceived and expressed with point.'—*Pall Mall Gazette.*

'The love incident is exquisite and exquisitely told. "Rosy" lives; her emotions stir us. Wonderfully suggested in several parts of the work is the severe irony of nature before profound human suffering. But the charm of the book is the analysis of mental torture, of interesting remorse, of the despair of one to whom the future is without light. One is grateful for the artistic revelation of the sweet wormwood of pain.'—*Saturday Review.*

Second Edition.

THE GREAT GOD PAN AND THE INMOST LIGHT. By ARTHUR MACHEN. Crown 8vo, 3s. 6d. net.

'Since Mr. Stevenson played with the crucibles of science in "Dr. Jekyll and Mr. Hyde" we have not encountered a more successful experiment of the sort.'—*Pall Mall Gazette.*

'Nothing so appalling as these tales has been given to publicity within our remembrance; in which, nevertheless, such ghastly fictions as Poe's "Telltale Heart," Bulwer's "The House and the Brain," and Le Fanu's "In a Glass Darkly" still are vividly present. The supernatural element is utilised with extraordinary power and effectiveness in both these blood-chilling masterpieces.'—*Daily Telegraph.*

'Will arouse the sort of interest that was created by "Dr. Jekyll and Mr. Hyde." The tales present a frankly impossible horror, which, nevertheless, kindles the imagination and excites a powerful curiosity. It is almost a book of genius, and we are not sure that the safeguarding adverb is not superfluous.'—*Birmingham Post.*

'The coarser terrors of Edgar Allen Poe do not leave behind them the shudder that one feels at the shadowed devil-mysteries of "The Great God Pan."'—*Liverpool Mercury.*

Fifth Edition.

DISCORDS. By GEORGE EGERTON. Crown 8vo, 3s. 6d. net.

'She has given, times without number, examples of her ripening power that astonish us. Her themes astound; her audacity is tremendous. In the many great passages an advance is proved that is little short of amazing.'—*Literary World.*

'A series of undoubtedly clever stories, told with a poetic dreaminess which softens the rugged truths of which they treat. Mothers might benefit themselves and convey help to young girls who are about to be married by the perusal of its pages.'—*Liverpool Mercury.*

'The book is true to human nature, for the author has genius, and, let us add, has heart. It is representative; it is, in the hackneyed phrase, a human document.'—*Speaker.*

'It is another note in the great chorus of revolt . . . on the whole clearer, more eloquent, and braver than almost any I have yet heard.'— T. P. ('Book of the Week'), *Weekly Sun,* December 30.

'What an absorbing, wonderful book it is: How absolutely sincere, and how finely wrong! George Egerton may be what the indefatigable Mr. Zangwill calls a one-I'd person, but she is a literary artist of exceptional endowment—probably a genius.'—*Woman.*

'She has many fine qualities. Her work throbs with temperament, and here and there we come upon touches that linger in the memory as of things felt and seen, not read of.'—*Daily News.*

PRINCE ZALESKI. By M. P. SHIEL. Crown 8vo, 3s. 6d. net.

'Mr. M. P. Shiel has in this volume produced something which is always rare, and which is every year becoming a greater rarity—a work of literary invention characterised by substantial novelty. We have Poe's analysis and Poe's glamour, but they are no longer distinct; they are combined in a new synthesis which stamps a new imaginative impression. A finely-wrought structure in which no single line impairs the symmetry and proportion. One of the most boldly-planned and strikingly-executed stories of its kind which has appeared for many a long day. We believe there is nothing in "Prince Zaleski" which that great inventor and masterly manipulator of the spoils of invention (Poe) would have disdained to father.'—*Daily Chronicle.*

'The Prince was a Sherlock Holmes, with this difference: that while yielding nothing to Conan Doyle's hero in mere intellectual agility, he had that imaginative insight which makes poets more frequently than detectives. Sherlock Holmes was a clever but essentially commonplace man. Prince Zaleski was a great man, simply. Enthralling . . . once begun they insist on being finished. Broadly and philosophically conceived, and put together with rare narrative skill, and feeling for effect.' —*Woman.*

'He has imparted to the three tales in this volume something of that atmosphere of eerie fantasy which Poe knew how to conjure, proceeding by the analysis of a baffling intricacy of detail to an unforeseen conclusion. The themes and their treatment are alike highly imaginative.'—*Daily News.*

'Manifestly written by one of Poe's true disciples. His analytical skill is not that of the detective, even of so brilliant a detective as Mr. Sherlock Holmes. Probably his exploits will interest the public far less than did those of Mr. Doyle's famous character; but the select few, who can appreciate delicate work, will delight in them exceedingly.'—*Speaker.*

Twenty-second Edition.

THE WOMAN WHO DID. By GRANT ALLEN. Crown 8vo, 3s. 6d. net.

' Really impressive ; but unfortunately—or fortunately, as we think it—it is a strong and impressive plea for what Mr. Grant Allen regards as the effete, unintelligent, utterly wrong view of things.'—*Spectator.*

'There is not a sensual thought or suggestion throughout the whole volume. Though I dislike and disbelieve in his gospel, I thoroughly respect Mr. Grant Allen for having stated it so honourably and so bravely.' —*Academy.*

' Even its bitterest enemies must surely feel some thrill of admiration for its courage. It is, once more, one philosopher against the world. Not in our day, perhaps, can it be decided which is right, Mr. Grant Allen, or the world. Perhaps our children's children will some day be canonising Mr. Grant Allen for the very book for which to-day he stands a much greater chance of being stoned, and happy lovers of the new era bless the name of the man who, almost single-handed, fought the battle of Free Love. Time alone can say. . . . None but the most foolish or malignant reader of 'The Woman Who Did' can fail to recognise the noble purpose which animates its pages. . . Label it as one will, it remains a clever, stimulating book. A real enthusiasm for humanity blazes through every page of this, in many ways, remarkable and significant little book.'—*Sketch.*

' Mr. Grant Allen has undoubtedly produced an epoch-making book, and one which will be a living voice when most of the novels of this generation have passed away into silence. It is epoch-making in the sense that "Uncle Tom's Cabin" was ;—the literary merits of that work were by no means great, but yet it rang like a tocsin through the land, arousing mankind to a sense of the slavery under which a large portion of humanity suffered. —*Humanitarian.*

WOMEN'S TRAGEDIES. By H. D. LOWRY. Crown 8vo, 3s. 6d. net.

' Written in a clear unaffected style, and with the restraint in handling delicate subjects that marks the true artist.'—*Athenæum.*

' Of that best and finest kind of imaginative realism which presents not only the object, but its surrounding atmosphere, there have of late been few more arresting and impressive examples than these tales of lowly Cornish life.'—*Academy.*

' He is the master of a style singularly strenuous and sensitive. What he sees he can express with marvellous vividness. There is nothing more terrible and perfect of its kind than his story, "The Man in the Room." It is magnificently done, powerfully imagined, and convincingly presented.' —*Black and White.*

' Mr. Lowry's "Women's Tragedies" are the most striking thumbnail sketches since Mr. Quiller Couch idly ceased to write his wonderful "Noughts and Crosses."'—*Star.*

' A wide and critical section of the reading public will be ready to welcome "Women's Tragedies." The author has not a little of the ancient mariner's power. He creates a situation which holds the reader mentally spellbound, and leaves an impression not readily effaced . . . sombre, even eerie, they prove, and yet strong with the author's power to fascinate.'—*Dundee Advertiser.*

GREY ROSES. By HENRY HARLAND. Crown 8vo, 3s. 6d.
net.

'Exceedingly pleasant to read. You close the book with a feeling that
you have met a host of charming people. "Castles Near Spain" comes
near to being a perfect thing of its kind.'—*Pall Mall Gazette.*

'They are charming stories, simple, full of freshness, with a good deal of
delicate wit, both in the imagining and in the telling. The last story of
the book, in spite of improbabilities quite tremendous, is a delightful story.
He has realised better than any one else the specialised character of the
short story and how it should be written.'—*Daily Chronicle.*

'Really delightful. "Castles near Spain" is as near perfection as it
could well be.'—*Spectator.*

'"Castles near Spain" as a fantastic love episode is simply inimitable,
and "Mercedes" is instinct with a pretty humour and child-like tenderness
that render it peculiarly—nay, uniquely—fascinating. "Grey Roses" are
entitled to rank among the choicest flowers of the realms of romance.'—
Daily Telegraph.

AT THE FIRST CORNER, AND OTHER STORIES. By
H. B. MARRIOTT WATSON. Crown 8vo, 3s. 6d. net.

'We willingly bear witness to Mr. Watson's brilliance, versatility, and
literary power. "An Ordeal of Three" is a fancy that is full of beauty and
delicate charm. When, again, Mr. Watson deals with the merely sordid and
real side of East-end London he justifies his choice by a certain convincing
realism which is never dull, and which is always inevitably true.'—*Pall
Mall Gazette.*

'A collection of nine stories admirably told by a master who has been
much copied but never equalled. Mr. Marriott Watson has all the qualities
of strength, imagination, and style, combined with a very complete sense
of proportion.'—*Vanity Fair.*

'Mr. Marriott Watson can write, and in these new stories he shows, more
manifestly than in any previous work, his capacity for dramatic realisation.
"An Ordeal of Three" has not only strength but charm.'—*Daily Chronicle.*

'Admirably conceived and brilliantly finished; the book will be read.'—
Saturday Review.

MONOCHROMES. By ELLA D'ARCY. Crown 8vo, 3s. 6d. net.

'If Miss D'Arcy can maintain this level, her future is secure. She has produced one story which comes near to being a masterpiece.'—*Daily Chronicle.*

'The cleverest volume of short stories that the year has given us.'—Mr. ZANGWILL in the *Pall Mall Magazine.*

'We doubt if any other living woman-writer could have written quite so well.'—*Saturday Review.*

'It is rare indeed to meet, in English, with a number of short stories of such distinction from an English pen.'—*Graphic.*

'She expresses herself with remarkable force and point, whilst her polished refinement of style gives literary value to these clever sketches. "Monochromes" is distinctly clever, and so well written as to give us strong hopes of its author's future.'—*Speaker.*

AT THE RELTON ARMS. By EVELYN SHARP. Crown 8vo, 3s. 6d. net.

'Miss Evelyn Sharp is to be congratulated on having, through the mouth of one of her characters, said one of the wisest words yet spoken on what is rather absurdly called "The Marriage Question" (page 132). It is an interesting and well-written story, with some smart characterisation and quite a sufficiency of humour.'—*Daily Chronicle.*

'A delightful story. The most genuine piece of humour in a book that is nowhere devoid of it, is that scene in the inn parlour where Digby finds himself engaged to two young women within five minutes ; while the two brief colloquies of the landlady and her cronies make one suspect that the author could produce an admirable study of village humour.'—*Athenæum.*

'A distinctly clever book, of a fresh conventionality.'—*Academy.*

'A brilliantly-written tale. . . . Teems with character sketches of extraordinary force and delicacy.'—*Daily Telegraph.*

Second Edition.

THE GIRL FROM THE FARM. By Gertrude Dix. Crown 8vo, 3s. 6d. net.

'Miss Dix has a pleasant and graceful style. The dean is well and sympathetically portrayed, and some of the scenes between him and Katherine bear the stamp of truth.'—*Daily Chronicle.*

'The novel is exceptionally well written, the characters are admirably drawn; there is a vividness, too, about several of the descriptions and scenes which is a great deal more than mere patient realism.'—*Glasgow Herald.*

'A decidedly clever little book.'—*Saturday Review.*

'The work of a writer with real gifts for fiction, gifts of characterisation and story-telling.'—*Star.*

'The story is cleverly constructed and well written.'—*Weekly Scotsman.*

'A thoroughly wholesome book and very clever. Katherine is a charming character.'—*Queen.*

'A powerful piece of writing. The dean and his daughter are drawn in masterly fashion.'—*Whitehall Review.*

THE MIRROR OF MUSIC. By Stanley V. Makower. Crown 8vo, 3s. 6d. net.

'It is a new thing in literature. There is a magnificent breadth, a simple directness, about the conception of this diary, and the leading idea is worked out with a resourceful ingenuity, a piercing insight, and an unerring taste which betray the hand of some one very like a master.'—*Woman.*

'A remarkably original and noteworthy book.'—*Saturday Review.*

'A fantastic and original book, to which belongs that note of distinction rare in the days of crude and rapid production.'—*Daily News.*

'The volume is a very remarkable one, and will be valued most of all by those who love music in its best and noblest forms.'—*Western Morning News.*

YELLOW AND WHITE.   By W. CARLTON DAWE.
Crown 8vo, 3s. 6d. net.

'Stirring and admirably written stories. In "Fan-Tan" a superb word-picture is painted of the Chinese national game, and of the gambling hells in which it is continuously played.   The stories abound in dramatic situations and palpitate with dramatic interest.'—*Daily Telegraph.*

'Are well written, and have about them a flavour of the shiny East, which would seem to show that they are the work of "one who knows" what he is talking about.'—*Daily Chronicle.*

'This thoroughly entertaining volume.   Rich in local colour, and presented with considerable literary skill in a peculiarly vivid and impressive manner.'—*Observer.*

'Are as idyllic and charming as the heart could desire.   Every page gives sign that the book has been put together with fastidious and loving care.   Several of the tales are completely effective, and none fall short of an entrancing picturesqueness.'—*Woman.*

THE MOUNTAIN LOVERS.   By FIONA MACLEOD.
Crown 8vo, 3s. 6d. net.

'It is impossible to read her and not to feel that some magic in her touch has made the sun seem brighter, the grass greener, the world more wonderful.'—Mr. GEORGE COTTERELL in *The Academy.*

'We eagerly devour page after page; we are taken captive by the speed and poetry of the book.'—*Literary World.*

'Primitive instincts and passions, primitive superstitions and faiths, are depicted with a passionate sympathy that acts upon us as an irresistible charm.'—*National Observer.*

'From Nial the Soulless, with his hopeless quest and wild songs and incantations, to sweet Sorcha, who dies of the dream in her eyes, these mountain folk have charm to set one musing. The book is altogether fascinating.'—*Saturday Review.*

'The sadness of Fiona Macleod's "Mountain Lovers" is well redeemed by the art with which the short and simple story is told.'—*St. James's Gazette.*

Third Edition.

THE WOMAN WHO DIDN'T. By VICTORIA CROSSE.
Crown 8vo, 3s. 6d. net.

'No one who recollects "Theodora" will need to be told with what acute perception the author reveals the hidden springs of human conduct. In her the feminine gift of intuition seems to be developed with almost uncanny strength, and what she sees she has the power of flashing upon her readers with wonderful vividness and felicity of phrase. Readers will find within its pages a strong and subtle study of feminine nature, biting irony, restrained passion, and a style that is both forcible and polished.'— *Speaker.*

'A striking, well-told story, strong in character drawing, subtle in observation, and fascinating in its hold of the reader.'—*Realm.*

'Is undoubtedly effective. Told with singular force and naturalness, which renders it by no means unworthy of the admirable series in which it is included.'—*Whitehall Review.*

'Is at least a proof that the "Keynotes Series" can touch the soft pedal of resignation as well as the clarion of revolt.'—*Sketch.*

THE THREE IMPOSTORS. By ARTHUR MACHEN.
Crown 8vo, 3s. 6d. net.

'With this new volume Mr. Machen boldly challenges comparison with Mr. Stevenson's "Dynamiters." We enjoy his humour and marvel at his ingenuity.'—*Daily Chronicle.*

'We confess to having read the volume with entrancing interest. It has power, it has grip, it holds the reader; and if it leaves him in a decidedly creepy condition, it likewise leaves him asking, like Oliver Twist, for more.' —*Whitehall Review.*

'These different tales are ingeniously strung together, and lead up to a fearful climax. The idea is gracefully and artistically worked out. Those who enjoy a thrill of horror will find much entertainment in these weird and uncanny stories.'—*Scotsman.*

'Remarkably well done and remarkably thrilling. Mr. Machen has constructed a book full of trepidations and unnamed terrors. It is not Stevenson, of course, but it is a prodigiously clever counterfeit.'—*Woman.*

Second Edition.

THE BRITISH BARBARIANS. By GRANT ALLEN.
Crown 8vo, 3s. net.

'Mr. Allen takes occasion to say a good many things that require saying, and suggests a good many reforms that would, if adopted, bring our present legal code more into harmony with modern humanity and the exigencies of its development.'—*Saturday Review.*

'A clever, trenchant satire on the petty conventionalities of modern life.'—*Vanity Fair.*

'All will acknowledge the skill and cleverness of the writing. Honest convictions, honestly stated, always merit attention, especially when they are presented in so clever and skilful a dress.'—*Western Morning News.*

'We can warmly recommend it as an eminently readable and distinctly clever piece of work.'—*Publishers' Circular.*

'Is not a book to be dismissed lightly. There can be no doubt that Mr. Grant Allen is sincere in what he here expounds, and if for no other reason, "The British Barbarians" at least deserves consideration.'—*Academy.*

'It is a triumph of the advocate's art, so advanced, so honest, and so fearless.'—*Queen.*

NOBODY'S FAULT. By NETTA SYRETT. Crown 8vo, 3s. 6d. net.

'An extremely careful and clever study . . . a deeply interesting story.—*Daily Chronicle.*

'The latest volume of the Keynotes Series is one of the pleasantest of the lot. The "modern" ideas of all the characters are the ideas which reasonable people are beginning to hold, and they are propounded not in a scream, but in the level conversational tones in which reasonable people would speak them.'—*Pall Mall Gazette.*

'Yet another success in Mr. Lane's "Keynotes" Series. "Nobody's Fault" is an exceedingly clever novel, and we shall expect to hear of its authoress again. It reads like a transcript from a personal experience. One follows Bridget's career with almost breathless interest.'—*Weekly Sun.*

'Bridget is alive to the finger tips; a vivid, impulsive creature; of as many moods as there are hours in the day; brave, beautiful, outspoken, with something of temperament genius.'—*Daily News.*

PLATONIC AFFECTIONS. By John Smith. Crown 8vo, 3s. 6d. net.

'A remarkably powerful and original story.'—*Daily Telegraph.*

'The reader will not feel inclined to quarrel with Mr. Smith for the light and breezy way in which he deals with the problem: therein lies much of the charm of " Platonic Affections." '—*Academy.*

'An original and striking story, written in easy and pleasant style. Original, since though there is nothing new in the fact that "platonic" arrangements never stand the test of time, the inevitable *dénouement* of the impossible problem that two deliciously honest people try to solve, is worked out so delicately, and with such subtle understanding of human, especially feminine, nature, that the story is really a fascinating, as well as an interesting study.'—*Pall Mall Gazette.*

WHERE THE ATLANTIC MEETS THE LAND. By Caldwell Lipsett. Crown 8vo, 3s. 6d. net.

' "The Unforgiven Sin," a story of woman's dishonour judged in the fierce light of Irish peasant opinion, is an exceedingly strong piece of work, restrained, dignified, and imaginative.'—*Sketch.*

'We shall look with expectant pleasure for so promising a writer's next volume.'—*Glasgow Herald.*

'It is quite a relief to meet with a teller of the short story to whom, within the bounds he has set himself, one is justified in giving almost unstinted praise.'—*Morning Post.*

IN HOMESPUN. By E. Nesbit. Crown 8vo, 3s. 6d. net.

'Short as they are . . . they are really literature "In Homespun," and hardly contain a line which does not add to the effect of the tale, which is told with much simple and homely force.'—*Spectator.*

'Wherever we turn to in "In Homespun" we discover reasons for applause, and we can safely recommend Mrs. Nesbit's contribution to the "Keynotes Series" as one of the most refreshing.'—*Literary World.*

' "A Death-bed Confession" is one of the strongest, sternest stories which have appeared in print for many a year past. "Coals of Fire" is fine enough itself to make the fortune of the book.'—*Daily Telegraph.*

NETS FOR THE WIND. By Una Taylor. Crown 8vo, 3s. 6d. net.

'Miss Taylor is to be congratulated upon a very remarkable achievement. One thing is certain, that she can write very beautifully and brilliantly.'—*Glasgow Herald.*

'Full of fascination. The writer is an artist in words and the word painting is always finished like a picture.'—*Scotsman.*

'Wild, fantastic, and full of dreamy sadness, are the sketches in this volume.'—*Pall Mall Gazette.*

'Miss Taylor has imagination and also a picturesque and delicately vivid style.'—*Daily News.*

IN SCARLET AND GREY: Stories of Soldiers and Others. By Florence Henniker. With 'The Spectre of the Real.' By Florence Henniker and Thomas Hardy. Crown 8vo, 3s. 6d. net.

'The work of a keen and sympathetic observer of life endowed with a simple and graphic literary style. They are realistic in the true sense of the word, and are full of a deep though restrained pathos.'—*Pall Mall Gazette.*

'A collection of profoundly melancholy stories which nevertheless make extremely agreeable reading.'—*Graphic.*

'Each of these stories can be read with pleasure both for its literary form and on account of its own intrinsic interest as a tale.'—*Gentlewoman.*

'Written with quiet pathos, unerring insight, and conspicuous felicity of expression.'—*Leeds Mercury.*

'It is a real delight to read anything so delicately finished and so rich in thoughtful insight as are these stories.'—*Speaker.*

DAY BOOKS. By Mabel E. Wotton. Crown 8vo, 3s. 6d. net.

'The interest is considerable and well sustained.'—*Whitehall Review.*

'Stamp her as a keen analyst of character and motive, and a writer who can be graceful or powerful as the occasion requires.'—*Scotsman.*

'"Morison's Heir" is a really clever study of a shallow and selfish woman. The irony of a delicate situation is skilfully developed.'—*Glasgow Herald.*

FORTHCOMING VOLUMES.

STELLA MARIS.   By MARIE CLOTHILDE BALFOUR.

UGLY IDOL.   By CLAUD NICHOLSON.

SHAPES IN THE FIRE.   By M. P. SHIEL.

KAKEMONOS.   By W. CARLTON DAWE.

GOD'S FAILURES.   By J. S. FLETCHER.

JOHN LANE

THE ✠
BODLEY
HEAD ✠
VIGO Sᵗ
W. ✠✠
Telegrams
"BODLEIAN
LONDON"

CATALOGUE *of* PUBLICATIONS
in BELLES LETTRES *all at net prices*

List of Books

IN

BELLES LETTRES

Published by John Lane

𝕿𝖍𝖊 𝕭𝖔𝖉𝖑𝖊𝖞 𝕳𝖊𝖆𝖉

VIGO STREET, LONDON, W.

Adams (Francis).
ESSAYS IN MODERNITY. Crown 8vo.
5s. net. [*Shortly.*
A CHILD OF THE AGE. (*See* KEY-
NOTES SERIES.)

A. E.
HOMEWARD SONGS BY THE WAY.
Sq. 16mo, wrappers. 1s. 6d. net.
*Transferred to the present Pub-
lisher.* [*Second Edition.*

Aldrich (T. B.)
LATER LYRICS. Sm. Fcap. 8vo.
2s. 6d. net.

Allen (Grant).
THE LOWER SLOPES: A Volume of
Verse. With Title-page and Cover
Design by J. ILLINGWORTH KAY.
Crown 8vo. 5s. net.
THE WOMAN WHO DID. (*See* KEY-
NOTES SERIES.)
THE BRITISH BARBARIANS. (*See*
KEYNOTES SERIES.)

Arcady Library (The).
A Series of Open-Air Books. Edited
by J. S. FLETCHER. With Cover
Designs by PATTEN WILSON.
Each volume crown 8vo. 5s. net.
  I. ROUND ABOUT A BRIGHTON
    COACH OFFICE. By MAUDE
    EGERTON KING. With
    over 30 Illustrations by
    LUCY KEMP-WELCH.
  II. LIFE IN ARCADIA. By J. S.
    FLETCHER. Illustrated by
    PATTEN WILSON.

Arcady Library (The)—*cont.*
  III. SCHOLAR GIPSIES. By JOHN
    BUCHAN. With 7 full-page
    Etchings by D.Y. CAMERON
The following is in preparation :
  IV. IN THE GARDEN OF PEACE.
    By HELEN MILMAN. With
    Illustrations by EDMUND
    H. NEW.

Beeching (Rev. H. C.).
IN A GARDEN : Poems. With Title-
page designed by ROGER FRY.
Crown 8vo. 5s. net.
ST. AUGUSTINE AT OSTIA. Crown
8vo, wrappers. 1s. net.

Beerbohm (Max).
THE WORKS OF MAX BEERBOHM.
With a Bibliography by JOHN
LANE. Sq. 16mo. 4s. 6d. net.

Benson (Arthur Christopher)
LYRICS. Fcap. 8vo, buckram. 5s.
net.
LORD VYET AND OTHER POEMS.
Fcap. 8vo. 3s. 6d. net.

**Bodley Head Anthologies
(The).**
Edited by ROBERT H. CASE. With
Title-page and Cover Designs by
WALTER WEST. Each volume
crown 8vo. 5s. net.
  I. ENGLISH EPITHALAMIES.
    By ROBERT H. CASE.

Bodley Head Anthologies (The)—*continued.*

    II. MUSA PISCATRIX. By JOHN BUCHAN. With 6 Etchings by E. PHILIP PIMLOTT.

    III. ENGLISH ELEGIES. By JOHN C BAILEY.

    IV. ENGLISH SATIRES. By CHAS. HILL DICK.

Bridges (Robert).

SUPPRESSED CHAPTERS AND OTHER BOOKISHNESS. Crown 8vo. 3s. 6d. net.   [*Second Edition.*

Brotherton (Mary).

ROSEMARY FOR REMEMBRANCE. With Title-page and Cover Design by WALTER WEST. Fcap. 8vo. 3s. 6d. net.

Crackanthorpe (Hubert).

VIGNETTES. A Miniature Journal of Whim and Sentiment. Fcap. 8vo, boards. 2s. 6d. net.

Crane (Walter).

TOY BOOKS. Re-issue, each with new Cover Design and End Papers. This LITTLE PIG'S PICTURE BOOK, containing :

    I. THIS LITTLE PIG.

    II. THE FAIRY SHIP.

    III. KING LUCKIEBOY'S PARTY.

The three bound in one volume with a decorative cloth cover, end papers, and a newly written and designed preface and title-page. 3s. 6d. net ; separately 9d. net each.

    MOTHER HUBBARD'S PICTURE BOOK, containing :

    I. MOTHER HUBBARD'S.

    II. THE THREE BEARS.

    III. THE ABSURD A. B. C.

The three bound in one volume with a decorative cloth cover, end papers, and a newly written and designed preface and title-page. 3s. 6d. net ; separately 9d. net each.

Custance (Olive).

FIRST FRUITS : Poems. Fcap. 8vo. 3s. 6d. net.

Dalmon (C. W.).

SONG FAVOURS. With a Title-page by J. P. DONNE. Sq. 16mo, 3s. 6d. net.

Davidson (John).

PLAYS : An Unhistorical Pastoral ; A Romantic Farce : Bruce, a Chronicle Play ; Smith, a Tragic Farce ; Scaramouch in Naxos, a Pantomime. With a Frontispiece and Cover Design by AUBREY BEARDSLEY. Small 4to. 7s. 6d. net.

FLEET STREET ECLOGUES. Fcap 8vo, buckram. 4s. 6d. net.
                    [*Third Edition.*

FLEET STREET ECLOGUES. 2nd Series. Fcap. 8vo, buckram. 4s. 6d. net.   [*Second Edition.*

A RANDOM ITINERARY AND A BALLAD. With a Frontispiece and Title-page by LAURENCE HOUSMAN. Fcap. 8vo, Irish Linen. 5s. net.

BALLADS AND SONGS. With a Title-page and Cover Design by WALTER WEST. Fcap. 8vo, buckram. 5s. net.   [*Fourth Edition.*

NEW BALLADS. Fcap. 8vo, buckram. 4s. 6d. net.

De Tabley (Lord)

POEMS, DRAMATIC AND LYRICAL. By JOHN LEICESTER WARREN (Lord de Tabley). Illustrations and Cover Design by C. S. RICKETTS. Crown 8vo. 7s. 6d. net.   [*Third Edition.*

POEMS, DRAMATIC AND LYRICAL. Second Series, uniform in binding with the former volume. Crown 8vo. 5s. net.

Duer (Caroline, and Alice).

POEMS. Fcap. 8vo. 3s. 6d. net.

Egerton (George)

KEYNOTES. (*See* KEYNOTES SERIES.)

DISCORDS. (*See* KEYNOTES SERIES.)

YOUNG OFEG'S DITTIES. A translation from the Swedish of OLA HANSSON. With Title-page and Cover Design by AUBREY BEARDSLEY. Crown 8vo. 3s. 6d. net.

SYMPHONIES.   [*In preparation.*

Eglinton (John).

TWO ESSAYS ON THE REMNANT. Post 8vo, wrappers. 1s. 6d net. *Transferred to the present Publisher.* [*Second Edition.*

Eve's Library.

Each volume, crown 8vo. 3s. 6d. net.

I. MODERN WOMEN. An English rendering of LAURA MARHOLM HANSSON'S "DAS BUCH DER FRAUEN" by HERMIONE RAMSDEN. Subjects: Sonia Kovalevsky, George Egerton, Eleanora Duse, Amalie Skram, Marie Bashkirtseff, A. Ch. Edgren Leffler.

II. THE ASCENT OF WOMAN. By ROY DEVEREUX.

III. MARRIAGE QUESTIONS IN MODERN FICTION. By ELIZABETH RACHEL CHAPMAN.

Fea (Allan).

THE FLIGHT OF THE KING : a full, true, and particular account of the escape of His Most Sacred Majesty King Charles II. after the Battle of Worcester, with Twelve Portraits in Photogravure and nearly 100 other Illustrations. Demy 8vo. 21s. net.

Field (Eugene).

THE LOVE AFFAIRS OF A BIBLIOMANIAC. Post 8vo. 3s. 6d. net.

Fletcher (J. S.).

THE WONDERFUL WAPENTAKE. By "A SON OF THE SOIL." With 18 full-page Illustrations by J. A. SYMINGTON. Crown 8vo. 5s. 6d. net.

LIFE IN ARCADIA. (*See* ARCADY LIBRARY.)

GOD'S FAILURES. (*See* KEYNOTES SERIES.)

BALLADS OF REVOLT. Sq. 32mo. 2s. 6d. net.

Ford (James L.).

THE LITERARY SHOP AND OTHER TALES. Fcap. 8vo. 3s. 6d. net.

Four-and-Sixpenny Novels

Each volume with Title-page and Cover Design by PATTEN WILSON. Crown 8vo. 4s. 6d. net.

GALLOPING DICK. By H. B. MARRIOTT WATSON.

THE WOOD OF THE BRAMBLES. By FRANK MATHEW.

THE SACRIFICE OF FOOLS. By R. MANIFOLD CRAIG.

A LAWYER'S WIFE. By Sir NEVILL GEARY, Bart. [*Second Edition.*

The following are in preparation :

WEIGHED IN THE BALANCE. By HARRY LANDER.

GLAMOUR. By META ORRED.

PATIENCE SPARHAWK AND HER TIMES. By GERTRUDE ATHERTON.

THE WISE AND THE WAYWARD. By G. S. STREET.

MIDDLE GREYNESS. By A. J. DAWSON.

THE MARTYR'S BIBLE. By GEORGE FIFTH.

A CELIBATE'S WIFE. By HERBERT FLOWERDEW.

MAX. By JULIAN CROSKEY.

Fuller (H. B.).

THE PUPPET BOOTH. Twelve Plays. Crown 8vo. 4s. 6d. net.

Gale (Norman).

ORCHARD SONGS. With Title-page and Cover Design by J. ILLINGWORTH KAY. Fcap. 8vo, Irish Linen. 5s. net. Also a Special Edition limited in number on hand-made paper bound in English vellum. £1 1s. net.

Garnett (Richard).

POEMS. With Title-page by J. ILLINGWORTH KAY. Crown 8vo. 5s. net.

DANTE, PETRARCH, CAMOENS, cxxiv Sonnets, rendered in English. With Title-page by PATTEN WILSON. Crown 8vo. 5s. net.

Gibson (Charles Dana).

PICTURES : Eighty-Five Large Cartoons. Oblong Folio. 15s. net.

PICTURES OF PEOPLE. Eighty-Five Large Cartoons. Oblong folio. 15s. net.

[*In preparation.*

Gosse (Edmund).

THE LETTERS OF THOMAS LOVELL
BEDDOES. Now first edited. Pott
8vo. 5s. net.
Also 25 copies large paper. 12s. 6d. net.

Grahame (Kenneth).

PAGAN PAPERS. With Title-page
by AUBREY BEARDSLEY. Fcap.
8vo. 5s. net.
[*Out of Print at present.*
THE GOLDEN AGE. With Cover
Design by CHARLES ROBINSON.
Crown 8vo. 3s. 6d. net.
[*Fifth Edition.*

Greene (G. A.).

ITALIAN LYRISTS OF TO-DAY.
Translations in the original metres
from about thirty-five living Italian
poets, with bibliographical and
biographical notes. Crown 8vo.
5s. net.

Greenwood (Frederick).

IMAGINATION IN DREAMS. Crown
8vo. 5s. net.

Hake (T. Gordon).

A SELECTION FROM HIS POEMS.
Edited by Mrs. MEYNELL. With
a Portrait after D. G. ROSSETTI,
and a Cover Design by GLEESON
WHITE. Crown 8vo. 5s. net.

Hayes (Alfred).

THE VALE OF ARDEN AND OTHER
POEMS. With a Title-page and a
Cover designed by E. H. NEW,
Fcap. 8vo. 3s. 6d. net.
Also 25 copies large paper. 15s. net.

Hazlitt (William).

LIBER AMORIS; OR, THE NEW
PYGMALION. Edited, with an
Introduction, by RICHARD LE
GALLIENNE. To which is added
an exact transcript of the original
MS., Mrs. Hazlitt's Diary in
Scotland, and letters never before
published. Portrait after BE-
WICK, and facsimile letters. 400
Copies only. 4to, 364 pp., buck-
ram. 21s. net.

Heinemann (William).

THE FIRST STEP; A Dramatic
Moment. Small 4to. 3s. 6d. net.

Hopper (Nora).

BALLADS IN PROSE. With a Title-
page and Cover by WALTER
WEST. Sq. 16mo. 5s. net.
UNDER QUICKEN BOUGHS. With
Title-page designed by PATTEN
WILSON, and Cover designed by
ELIZABETH NAYLOR. Crown
8vo. 5s. net.

Housman (Clemence).

THE WERE WOLF. With 6 full-
page Illustrations, Title-page,
and Cover Design by LAURENCE
HOUSMAN. Sq. 16mo. 3s. 6d.
net.

Housman (Laurence).

GREEN ARRAS: Poems. With 6
Illustrations, Title-page, Cover
Design, and End Papers by the
Author. Crown 8vo. 5s. net.
GODS AND THEIR MAKERS. Crown
8vo, 5s. net. [*In preparation.*

Irving (Laurence).

GODEFROI AND YOLANDE: A Play.
Sm. 4to. 3s. 6d. net.
[*In preparation.*

James (W. P.)

ROMANTIC PROFESSIONS: A Volume
of Essays. With Title-page designed by J. ILLINGWORTH KAY.
Crown 8vo. 5s. net.

Johnson (Lionel).

THE ART OF THOMAS HARDY: Six
Essays. With Etched Portrait by
WM. STRANG, and Bibliography
by JOHN LANE. Crown 8vo.
5s. 6d. net. [*Second Edition.*
Also 150 copies, large paper, with proofs
of the portrait. £1 1s. net.

Johnson (Pauline).

WHITE WAMPUM: Poems. With a
Title-page and Cover Design by
E. H. NEW. Crown 8vo. 5s. net.

Johnstone (C. E.).

BALLADS OF BOY AND BEAK. With
a Title-page by F. H. TOWNSEND.
Sq. 32mo. 2s. net.

Keynotes Series.

Each volume with specially-designed Title-page by AUBREY BEARDS-LEY or PATTEN WILSON. Crown 8vo, cloth. 3s. 6d. net.

I. KEYNOTES. By GEORGE EGERTON.
[*Seventh Edition.*

II. THE DANCING FAUN. By FLORENCE FARR.

III. POOR FOLK. Translated from the Russian of F. Dostoievsky by LENA MILMAN. With a Preface by GEORGE MOORE.

IV. A CHILD OF THE AGE. By FRANCIS ADAMS.

V. THE GREAT GOD PAN AND THE INMOST LIGHT. By ARTHUR MACHEN.
[*Second Edition.*

VI. DISCORDS. By GEORGE EGERTON.
[*Fifth Edition.*

VII. PRINCE ZALESKI. By M. P. SHIEL.

VIII. THE WOMAN WHO DID. By GRANT ALLEN.
[*Twenty-second Edition.*

IX. WOMEN'S TRAGEDIES. By H. D. LOWRY.

X. GREY ROSES. By HENRY HARLAND.

XI. AT THE FIRST CORNER AND OTHER STORIES. By H. B. MARRIOTT WATSON.

XII. MONOCHROMES. By ELLA D'ARCY.

XIII. AT THE RELTON ARMS. By EVELYN SHARP.

XIV. THE GIRL FROM THE FARM. By GERTRUDE DIX.
[*Second Edition.*

XV. THE MIRROR OF MUSIC. By STANLEY V. MAKOWER.

XVI. YELLOW AND WHITE. By W. CARLTON DAWE.

XVII. THE MOUNTAIN LOVERS. By FIONA MACLEOD.

XVIII. THE WOMAN WHO DIDN'T. By VICTORIA CROSSE.
[*Third Edition.*

Keynotes Series—*continued.*

XIX. THE THREE IMPOSTORS. By ARTHUR MACHEN.

XX. NOBODY'S FAULT. By NETTA SYRETT.
[*Second Edition.*

XXI. THE BRITISH BARBARIANS. By GRANT ALLEN.
[*Second Edition.*

XXII. IN HOMESPUN. By E. NESBIT.

XXIII. PLATONIC AFFECTIONS. By JOHN SMITH.

XXIV. NETS FOR THE WIND. By UNA TAYLOR.

XXV. WHERE THE ATLANTIC MEETS THE LAND. By CALDWELL LIPSETT.

XXVI. IN SCARLET AND GREY. By FLORENCE HENNIKER. (With THE SPECTRE OF THE REAL by FLORENCE HENNIKER and THOMAS HARDY.) [*Second Edition.*

XXVII. MARIS STELLA. By MARIE CLOTHILDE BALFOUR.

XXVIII. DAY BOOKS. By MABEL E. WOTTON.

XXIX. SHAPES IN THE FIRE. By M. P. SHIEL.

XXX. UGLY IDOL. By CLAUD NICHOLSON.

The following are in rapid preparation:

XXXI. KAKEMONOS. By W. CARLTON DAWE.

XXXII. GOD'S FAILURES. By J. S. FLETCHER.

XXXIII. A DELIVERANCE. By ALLAN MONKHOUSE.

XXXIV. MERE SENTIMENT. By A. J. DAWSON.

Lane's Library.

Each volume crown 8vo. 3s. 6d. net.

I. MARCH HARES. By GEORGE FORTH.
[*Second Edition.*

II. THE SENTIMENTAL SEX. By GERTRUDE WARDEN.

III. GOLD. By ANNIE LINDEN.

Lane's Library—*continued.*

The following are in preparation:

IV. BROKEN AWAY. By BEA-TRICE GRIMSHAW.

V. RICHARD LARCH. By E. A. BENNETT.

VI. THE DUKE OF LINDEN. By JOSEPH F. CHARLES.

Leather (R. K.).

VERSES. 250 copies. Fcap. 8vo. 3s. net. [*Transferred to the present Publisher.*

Lefroy (Edward Cracroft.)

POEMS. With a Memoir by W. A. GILL, and a reprint of Mr. J. A. SYMONDS' Critical Essay on "Echoes from Theocritus." Cr. 8vo. Photogravure Portrait. 5s. net.

Le Gallienne (Richard).

PROSE FANCIES. With Portrait of the Author by WILSON STEER. Crown 8vo. Purple cloth. 5s. net. [*Fourth Edition.*
Also a limited large paper edition. 12s. 6d. net.

THE BOOK BILLS OF NARCISSUS, An Account rendered by RICHARD LE GALLIENNE. With a Frontis-piece. Crown 8vo, purple cloth. 3s. 6d. net. [*Third Edition.*
Also 50 copies on large paper. 8vo. 10s. 6d. net.

ROBERT LOUIS STEVENSON, AN ELEGY, AND OTHER POEMS, MAINLY PERSONAL. With Etched Title-page by D. Y. CAMERON. Crown 8vo, purple cloth. 4s. 6d. net.
Also 75 copies on large paper. 8vo. 12s. 6d. net.

ENGLISH POEMS. Crown 8vo, pur-ple cloth. 4s. 6d. net.
[*Fourth Edition, revised.*

GEORGE MEREDITH: Some Char-acteristics. With a Bibliography (much enlarged) by JOHN LANE, portrait, &c. Crown 8vo, purple cloth. 5s. 6d. net.
[*Fourth Edition.*

Le Gallienne (Richard)—*continued.*

THE RELIGION OF A LITERARY MAN. Crown 8vo, purple cloth. 3s. 6d. net. [*Fifth Thousand.*
Also a special rubricated edition on hand-made paper. 8vo. 10s. 6d. net.

RETROSPECTIVE REVIEWS, A LITER-ARY LOG, 1891-1895. 2 vols. Crown 8vo, purple cloth. 9s. net.

PROSE FANCIES (Second Series). Crown 8vo, Purple cloth. 5s. net.

THE QUEST OF THE GOLDEN GIRL. Crown 8vo. 5s. net.
[*In preparation.*
See also HAZLITT, WALTON and COTTON.

Lowry (H. D.).

MAKE BELIEVE. Illustrated by CHARLES ROBINSON. Crown 8vo, gilt edges or uncut. 5s. net.
WOMEN'S TRAGEDIES. (*See* KEY-NOTES SERIES).

Lucas (Winifred).

UNITS: Poems. Fcap. 8vo. 3s. 6d. net.

Lynch (Hannah).

THE GREAT GALEOTO AND FOLLY OR SAINTLINESS. Two Plays, from the Spanish of José ECHE-GARAY, with an Introduction. Small 4to. 5s. 6d. net.

Marzials (Theo.).

THE GALLERY OF PIGEONS AND OTHER POEMS. Post 8vo. 4s. 6d. net. [*Transferred to the present Publisher.*

The Mayfair Set.

Each volume fcap. 8vo. 3s. 6d. net.
I. THE AUTOBIOGRAPHY OF A BOY. Passages selected by his friend G. S. STREET. With a Title-page designed by C. W. FURSE.
[*Fifth Edition.*
II. THE JONESES AND THE ASTERISKS. A Story in Monologue. By GERALD CAMPBELL. With a Title-page and 6 Illustrations by F. H. TOWNSEND.
[*Second Edition.*

The Mayfair Set—*continued*.

   III. SELECT CONVERSATIONS WITH AN UNCLE, NOW EXTINCT. By H. G. WELLS. With a Title-page by F. H. TOWNSEND.

   IV. FOR PLAIN WOMEN ONLY. By GEORGE FLEMING. With a Title-page by PATTEN WILSON.

   V. THE FEASTS OF AUTOLYCUS: THE DIARY OF A GREEDY WOMAN. Edited by ELIZABETH ROBINS PENNELL. With a Title-page by PATTEN WILSON.

   VI. MRS. ALBERT GRUNDY: OBSERVATIONS IN PHILISTIA. By HAROLD FREDERIC. With a Title-page by PATTEN WILSON.
               [Second Edition.

Meredith (George).

THE FIRST PUBLISHED PORTRAIT OF THIS AUTHOR, engraved on the wood by W. BISCOMBE GARDNER, after the painting by G. F. WATTS. Proof copies on Japanese vellum, signed by painter and engraver. £1 1s. net.

Meynell (Mrs.).

POEMS. Fcap. 8vo. 3s. 6d. net.
               [Fourth Edition.

THE RHYTHM OF LIFE AND OTHER ESSAYS. Fcap. 8vo. 3s. 6d. net.
               [Third Edition.

THE COLOUR OF LIFE AND OTHER ESSAYS. Fcap 8vo. 3s. 6d. net.   *[Second Edition.*

THE DARLING YOUNG. Fcap. 8vo. 3s. 6d. net.   *[In preparation.*

Miller (Joaquin).

THE BUILDING OF THE CITY BEAUTIFUL. Fcap. 8vo. With a Decorated Cover. 5s. net.

Money-Coutts (F. B.).

POEMS. With Title-page designed by PATTEN WILSON. Crown 8vo. 3s. 6d. net.

Monkhouse (Allan).

BOOKS AND PLAYS: A Volume of Essays on Meredith, Borrow, Ibsen, and others. Crown 8vo. 5s. net.

Nesbit (E.).

A POMANDER OF VERSE. With a Title-page and Cover designed by LAURENCE HOUSMAN. Crown 8vo. 5s. net.

IN HOMESPUN. (*See* KEYNOTES SERIES.)

Nettleship (J. T.).

ROBERT BROWNING: Essays and Thoughts. Crown 8vo. 5s. 6d. net.   *[Third Edition.*

Noble (Jas. Ashcroft).

THE SONNET IN ENGLAND AND OTHER ESSAYS. Title-page and Cover Design by AUSTIN YOUNG. Crown 8vo. 5s. net.
Also 50 copies large paper. 12s. 6d. net

Oppenheim (Michael).

A HISTORY OF THE ADMINISTRATION OF THE ROYAL NAVY, and of Merchant Shipping in relation to the Navy from MDIX to MDCLX, with an introduction treating of the earlier period. With Illustrations. Demy 8vo. 15s. net.

O'Shaughnessy (Arthur).

HIS LIFE AND HIS WORK. With Selections from his Poems. By LOUISE CHANDLER MOULTON. Portrait and Cover Design. Fcap. 8vo. 5s. net.

Oxford Characters.

A series of lithographed portraits by WILL ROTHENSTEIN, with text by F. YORK POWELL and others. 200 copies only, folio, buckram. £3 3s. net.

25 special large paper copies containing proof impressions of the portraits signed by the artist, £6 6s. net.

Peters (Wm. Theodore).

POSIES OUT OF RINGS. With Title-page by PATTEN WILSON. Sq. 16mo. 2s. 6d. net.

Pierrot's Library.

Each volume with Title-page, Cover and End Papers, designed by AUBREY BEARDSLEY. Sq. 16mo. 2s. net.

    I. PIERROT. By H. DE VERE STACPOOLE.
    II. MY LITTLE LADY ANNE. By Mrs. EGERTON CASTLE.
    III. SIMPLICITY. By A. T. G. PRICE.
    IV. MY BROTHER. By VINCENT BROWN.

The following are in preparation:

    V. DEATH, THE KNIGHT, AND THE LADY. By H. DE VERE STACPOOLE.
    VI. MR. PASSINGHAM. By THOMAS COBB.
    VII. TWO IN CAPTIVITY. By VINCENT BROWN.

Plarr (Victor).

IN THE DORIAN MOOD: Poems. With Title-page by PATTEN WILSON. Crown 8vo. 5s. net.

Radford (Dollie).

SONGS AND OTHER VERSES. With a Title-page by PATTEN WILSON. Fcap. 8vo. 4s. 6d. net.

Rhys (Ernest).

A LONDON ROSE AND OTHER RHYMES. With Title-page designed by SELWYN IMAGE. Crown 8vo. 5s. net.

Robertson (John M.).

ESSAYS TOWARDS A CRITICAL METHOD. (New Series.) Crown 8vo. 5s. net. [*In preparation.*

St. Cyres (Lord).

THE LITTLE FLOWERS OF ST. FRANCIS: A new rendering into English of the Fioretti di San Francesco. Crown 8vo. 5s. net. [*In preparation.*

Seaman (Owen).

THE BATTLE OF THE BAYS. Fcap. 8vo. 3s. 6d. net.

Sedgwick (Jane Minot).

SONGS FROM THE GREEK. Fcap. 8vo. 3s. 6d. net.

Setoun (Gabriel).

THE CHILD WORLD: Poems. Illustrated by CHARLES ROBINSON. Crown 8vo, gilt edges or uncut. 5s. net. [*In preparation.*

Sharp (Evelyn).

WYMPS: Fairy Tales. With Coloured Illustrations by MABEL DEARMER. Small 4to, decorated cover. 4s. 6d. net. [*In preparation.*

AT THE RELTON ARMS. (*See* KEYNOTES SERIES.)

Shore (Louisa).

POEMS. With an appreciation by FREDERIC HARRISON and a Portrait. Fcap. 8vo. 5s. net.

Short Stories Series.

Each volume Post 8vo. Coloured edges. 2s. 6d. net.

    I. THE HINT O' HAIRST. By MÉNIE MURIEL DOWIE.
    II. THE SENTIMENTAL VIKINGS. By R. V. RISLEY.
    III. SHADOWS OF LIFE. By Mrs. MURRAY HICKSON.

Stevenson (Robert Louis).

PRINCE OTTO. A Rendering in French by EGERTON CASTLE. With Frontispiece, Title-page, and Cover Design by D. Y. CAMERON. Crown 8vo. 7s. 6d. net.

Also 50 copies on large paper, uniform in size with the Edinburgh Edition of the Works.

A CHILD'S GARDEN OF VERSES. With over 150 Illustrations by CHARLES ROBINSON. Crown 8vo. 5s. net. [*Second Edition.*

Stoddart (Thos. Tod).

THE DEATH WAKE. With an Introduction by ANDREW LANG. Fcap. 8vo. 5s. net.

Street (G. S.).

EPISODES. Post 8vo. 3s. net.

MINIATURES AND MOODS. Fcap. 8vo. 3s. net. [*Both transferred to the present Publisher.*

QUALES EGO: A FEW REMARKS, IN PARTICULAR AND AT LARGE. Fcap. 8vo. 3s. 6d. net.

Street (G. S.)—*continued*.

THE AUTOBIOGRAPHY OF A BOY. (*See* MAYFAIR SET.)

THE WISE AND THE WAYWARD. (*See* FOUR - AND - SIXPENNY NOVELS.)

Swettenham (F. A.)

MALAY SKETCHES. With a Title-page and Cover Design by PATTEN WILSON. Crown 8vo. 5s. net. [*Second Edition.*

Tabb (John B.).

POEMS. Sq. 32mo. 4s. 6d. net.

Tennyson (Frederick).

POEMS OF THE DAY AND YEAR. With a Title-page designed by PATTEN WILSON. Crown 8vo. 5s. net.

Thimm (Carl A.).

A COMPLETE BIBLIOGRAPHY OF FENCING AND DUELLING, AS PRACTISED BY ALL EUROPEAN NATIONS FROM THE MIDDLE AGES TO THE PRESENT DAY. With a Classified Index, arranged Chronologically according to Languages. Illustrated with numerous Portraits of Ancient and Modern Masters of the Art. Title-pages and Frontispieces of some of the earliest works. Portrait of the Author by WILSON STEER, and Title page designed by PATTEN WILSON. 4to. 21s. net.

Thompson (Francis).

POEMS. With Frontispiece, Title-page, and Cover Design by LAURENCE HOUSMAN. Pott 4to. 5s. net. [*Fourth Edition.*

SISTER-SONGS: An Offering to Two Sisters. With Frontispiece, Title-page, and Cover Design by LAURENCE HOUSMAN. Pott 4to. 5s. net.

Thoreau (Henry David).

POEMS OF NATURE. Selected and edited by HENRY S. SALT and FRANK B. SANBORN, with a Title-page designed by PATTEN WILSON. Fcap. 8vo. 4s. 6d. net.

Traill (H. D.).

THE BARBAROUS BRITISHERS: A Tip-top Novel. With Title and Cover Design by AUBREY BEARDSLEY. Crown 8vo, wrapper. 1s. net.

FROM CAIRO TO THE SOUDAN FRONTIER. With Cover Design by PATTEN WILSON. Crown 8vo. 5s. net.

Tynan Hinkson (Katharine).

CUCKOO SONGS. With Title-page and Cover Design by LAURENCE HOUSMAN. Fcap. 8vo. 5s. net.

MIRACLE PLAYS. OUR LORD'S COMING AND CHILDHOOD. With 6 Illustrations, Title-page, and Cover Design by PATTEN WILSON. Fcap. 8vo. 4s. 6d. net.

Walton and Cotton.

THE COMPLEAT ANGLER. Edited by RICHARD LE GALLIENNE. Illustrated by EDMUND H. NEW. Crown 4to, decorated cover. 15s. net.

Also to be had in twelve 1s. parts.

Watson (Rosamund Marriott).

VESPERTILIA AND OTHER POEMS. With a Title-page designed by R. ANNING BELL. Fcap. 8vo. 4s. 6d. net.

A SUMMER NIGHT AND OTHER POEMS. New Edition. With a Decorative Title-page. Fcap. 8vo. 3s. net.

Watson (William).

THE FATHER OF THE FOREST AND OTHER POEMS. With New Photogravure Portrait of the Author Fcap. 8vo, buckram. 3s. 6d. net. [*Fifth Edition.*

ODES AND OTHER POEMS. Fcap. 8vo, buckram. 4s. 6d. net. [*Fourth Edition.*

THE ELOPING ANGELS: A Caprice Square 16mo, buckram. 3s. 6d. net. [*Second Edition.*

EXCURSIONS IN CRITICISM: being some Prose Recreations of a Rhymer. Crown 8vo, buckram. 5s. net. [*Second Edition.*

Watson (William)—*continued.*

THE PRINCE'S QUEST AND OTHER POEMS. With a Bibliographical Note added. Fcap. 8vo, buckram. 4s. 6d. net.   [*Third Edition.*

THE PURPLE EAST: A Series of Sonnets on England's Desertion of Armenia. With a Frontispiece after G. F. WATTS, R.A. Fcap. 8vo, wrappers. 1s. net.
    [*Third Edition.*

Watt (Francis).

THE LAW'S LUMBER ROOM. Fcap. 8vo. 3s. 6d. net.
    [*Second Edition.*

Watts-Dunton (Theodore).

POEMS. Crown 8vo. 5s. net.
    [*In preparation.*

There will also be an *Edition de Luxe* of this volume printed at the Kelmscott Press.

Wharton (H. T.)

SAPPHO. Memoir, Text, Selected Renderings, and a Literal Translation by HENRY THORNTON WHARTON. With 3 Illustrations in Photogravure, and a Cover designed by AUBREY BEARDSLEY. Fcap. 8vo. 7s. 6d. net.   [*Third Edition.*

THE YELLOW BOOK

An Illustrated Quarterly.

Pott 4to.   5s. net.

I. April 1894, 272 pp., 15 Illustrations.   [*Out of print.*

II. July 1894, 364 pp., 23 Illustrations.

III. October 1894, 280 pp., 15 Illustrations.

IV. January 1895, 285 pp., 16 Illustrations.

V. April 1895, 317 pp., 14 Illustrations.

VI. July 1895, 335 pp., 16 Illustrations.

VII. October 1895, 320 pp., 20 Illustrations.

VIII. January 1896, 406 pp., 26 Illustrations.

IX. April 1896, 256 pp., 17 Illustrations.

X. July 1896, 340 pp., 13 Illustrations.

www.ingramcontent.com/pod-product-compliance
Lightning Source LLC
Chambersburg PA
CBHW030811020726
47499CB00006B/1866